SON OF
ROSEMARY

WORKS BY IRA LEVIN

NOVELS
Son of Rosemary
Sliver
The Boys from Brazil
The Stepford Wives
This Perfect Day
Rosemary's Baby
A Kiss Before Dying

PLAYS
Footsteps
Cantorial
Break A Leg
Deathtrap
Veronica's Room
Dr. Cook's Garden
General Seeger
Critic's Choice
Interlock
No Time For Sergeants
(from the novel by Mac Hyman)

MUSICALS
Drat! The Cat!
(music by Milton Schafer)

www.IraLevin.org

IRA LEVIN'S
SON OF ROSEMARY

THE SEQUEL TO *ROSEMARY'S BABY*

BLACK STONE

PUBLISHING

Published in 2024 by Blackstone Publishing
Cover design by James T. Egan of Bookfly Design

Printed in the United States of America

ISBN 979-8-212-64251-4
Fiction / Horror

Version 1

Blackstone Publishing
31 Mistletoe Rd.
Ashland, OR 97520

www.BlackstonePublishing.com

TO
MIA FARROW

"The Bible makes it abundantly clear that Satan is real, and that he is very powerful. He is not a myth, nor is he just a projection of our minds as we attempt to explain the mysteries of evil. He is a malevolent spiritual power whose sole goal is to oppose the work of God."

—BILLY GRAHAM
Newsweek, November 13, 1995

There may be trouble ahead,
But while there's moonlight and music
And love and romance—
    Let's face the music and dance.

Before the fiddlers have fled,
Before they ask us to pay the bill
And while we still have the chance—
    Let's face the music and dance.

—IRVING BERLIN
"Let's Face the Music and Dance"
Follow the Fleet, 1936

ONE

1

In Manhattan, on the crisp, clear morning of Tuesday, November 9, 1999, Dr. Stanley Shand, a retired dentist twice divorced, leaves his apartment on Amsterdam Avenue for his daily constitutional. Though eighty-nine he walks vigorously, his plaid-capped head erect, his eyes bright. He is buoyed both by good health and a secret, a glorious secret that warms his every waking moment. He has been a participant—indeed, has recently become the last living participant—in a cosmic event thirty-three years in the making that is now within two months of its ultimate fruition.

At Broadway and Seventy-fourth Street an out-of-control taxi shoots across the sidewalk and squashes Dr. Shand against the wall of the Beacon Theater. He dies instantly.

In that same instant—a few seconds after 11:03 a.m.—in the Halsey-Bodein Nursing Home in Upper Montclair, New Jersey, the eyes of the patient in Room 215 open. They have been closed all the years the woman has been at H-B—since nineteen-seventy-something, as long as anyone there can remember.

A wizened black nurse massaging the woman's right arm shows extraordinary presence of mind. She gulps, draws breath, and goes on massaging. "Hi, baby," she says softly. "Nice to have you with us." The nameplate on her uniform reads CLARISE; above it hangs an I ♥ ANDY button. Freeing a hand, she gropes for the night-stand, jabs a push button.

The patient's eyes, staring upward, blink. Her lips purse, shiny with salve. She's in her fifties, pale and fine-boned. Her head, its graying auburn hair neatly brushed, rolls toward the side, her blue eyes pleading.

"You're going to be fine," Clarise tells her, jabbing the push button, jabbing again. "Don't you worry, you're getting better now." She lowers the woman's arm to the bed. "I'm going to get the doctor," she says. "Don't you worry. Be right back."

The woman watches her leave.

"*TIFFANY! Take off them fuckin' earphones! Get Atkinson! Two-fifteen opened her eyes! She's awake! Two-fifteen's awake!*"

What in God's name had happened?

She'd been sitting at the desk by the bedroom window, around seven in the evening, while Andy lay on the floor a few feet away watching TV. She was typing a letter home about moving to San Francisco, trying not to hear Kukla and Ollie and the damn coven chanting up a storm next door at Minnie and Roman's—and here she was in a sunny hospital room with an IV in one arm and a nurse massaging the other. Was Andy hurt too? Oh God, please not! Had there been some kind of disaster? Why didn't she remember *anything*?

She got the tip of her tongue out, licked her lips; minty ointment of some kind coated them. How long had she been asleep? A day? Two? Nothing hurt, yet she couldn't quite move. She worked at getting her throat cleared.

The nurse hurried in. "Doctor's coming," she said. "Stay cool."

Rosemary whispered, "Is . . . my son here?"

"No, just you. Talking! Praise the Lord!" The nurse drew a sleeve down Rosemary's arm, squeezed her hand, and moved to the foot of the bed. "Praise Jesus!"

Rosemary said, "What . . . happened?"

"Don't nobody know, baby. You been out like a light."

"How long?"

Clarise drew a blanket up about Rosemary's shoulders, frowning. She said, "I don't rightly know. I wasn't here when you came in. You ax the doctor." She smiled down at Rosemary, CLARISE with an I ♥ ANDY button.

"My son's name is Andy," Rosemary said, smiling back up at her. "Does the heart mean love?"

Clarise said, "That's right." She touched a finger to the round white button. "'I love Andy.' They been doing it for—for a while now. Different things. Like 'I love New York,' anything."

Rosemary said, "It's cute. I haven't seen it before."

A man in a white jacket excused himself through a few elderly people looking in at the doorway, a large man with ginger hair and a bushy ginger beard. Clarise turned, moving aside, as he came in and closed the door. "She's talking, and she can move her head."

"Hello, Miss Fountain!" the doctor said, coming to the bed, smiling at her through his ginger beard. He put his bag and a manila folder on a chair alongside. "I'm Dr. Atkinson," he said, turning down the side of the blanket. "This is great news." He took Rosemary's wrist with warm fingers and looked at his raised watch.

"What happened to me?" she asked. "How long have I been here?"

"In a moment," the doctor said, studying the watch. He looked as if under the beard he wasn't much older than she, somewhere in his mid-thirties. An ultramodern stethoscope hung like a slim chrome necktie against his jacket, a DR. ATKINSON nameplate on one side of it and an I ♥ ANDY button on the other—an Andy on the staff, she guessed, or a favorite patient. She'd try to get one for herself before she left.

Dr. Atkinson let go her wrist, smiling down at her. "So far, so good," he said. "Surprisingly so. Bear with me another minute, please. I want to make sure we're not going to lose you again, then I'll tell you as much as we know. Do you feel any pain?"

"No," she said.

"Good. Try to relax; I know it won't be easy."

It wasn't. *As much as we know . . .*

Meaning that there were things they didn't know . . .

And the name he had called her, *Miss Fountain . . .*

An icy hollow grew in her stomach—while the doctor attended to her heart and her eyes and her ears and her blood pressure.

She had been there *longer* than two days, she was sure of it. Two *weeks?*

They had cast a spell on her, Minnie and Roman and the rest of the coven. That was what the heavy chanting was about. They had found out she was taking Andy three thousand miles away from them, that she had bought the plane tickets.

She remembered how they had cast a spell on her old friend Hutch, back when she was pregnant, because they were afraid he knew enough about witchcraft, the real kind, to catch on to what they had done to her, and whose child she was carrying. Poor Hutch had been in an inexplicable coma for *three or four months*, and then died. She was lucky to be alive but what of *Andy?* He was completely in their hands while she lay there;

they'd be feeding and fostering the side of him she tried not to think about. "*Damn* them!" she said.

"I'm sorry, I didn't get that," the doctor said, seating himself at the bedside. He hitched the chair closer, leaned his gingery head toward her.

"How long?" she asked him. "Weeks? Months?"

"Miss Fountain—"

"Reilly," she said. "Rosemary Reilly."

He drew back, opened the folder on his lap, peered downward.

"Tell me!" she said. "I have a six-year-old son who's in—he's with people I don't trust."

"You were signed in here," Dr. Atkinson said, looking down, "by a Mr. and Mrs. Clarence Fountain, as their granddaughter, Rosemary Fountain."

"The Fountains," Rosemary said, "belong to the—to this group of people I'm talking about. They're the ones who put me here, I mean put me into the coma. Isn't that what it was, an `inexplicable coma'?"

"Yes, but a coma isn't—"

"I know what was done to me," she broke in, raising herself on an elbow; she fell back. She tried to raise herself again despite warnings and hands; this time she got the elbow back where she could brace herself against it. She stayed up, eye to eye with Dr. Atkinson. "I know what was done to me," she said, "but I'm not going to tell you because I know from experience that you'll think I'm crazy. I'm not. I'd appreciate it if you would please tell me how long I've been here, and where exactly I am, and when I'll be able to go home."

Dr. Atkinson sat back and drew a breath. He looked gravely at her. Said, "You're in a nursing home in Upper Montclair, New Jersey."

"A *nursing home?*" she said.

He nodded. "Halsey-Bodein. We specialize in—long-term care."

She stared at him. Said, "What day is this?"

"Tuesday," he said, "November ninth . . ."

"*November?*" she said. "It was May last night! Dear God!" She fell back against the pillow, both hands over her mouth, her eyes staring upward, tears welling. *May, June, July, August, September, October—six months!* Snatched from her life! And Andy in their hands all those six-times-thirty days and nights!

She saw the doctor still looking gravely at her, still keeping a distance. . . .

She raised her hands from her mouth, turned them before her eyes. Their backs, the skin of them, was—*grainy*. A brown spot, two . . . She touched one hand with the fingertips of the other. Looked at him.

"You've been here a very long time," he said. Now he leaned close, took her hand, and clasped it. Held it. Clarise, at the other side of the bed, took hold of her other hand. She looked from one of them to the other, her eyes wide, her lips trembling.

"Would you like a sedative?" the doctor asked.

She shook her head. "No," she said. "No. I don't want to sleep again. Ever. How old am I? What *year* is it?"

He swallowed, tears in his eyes. "It's—1999," he said.

She stared at him.

He nodded.

Clarise confirmed it, biting her lip, nodding.

"You were brought here in September of 1972," Dr. Atkinson said, blinking. "A little over twenty-seven years ago. Before that you'd been in New York Hospital for four months. The Fountains, whoever they were, set up a trust fund that's been paying for your maintenance here ever since."

She lay back, shut her eyes, shook her head. *Impossible! Impossible!* The coven had won! Andy was fully grown, a stranger raised by *them*, in their ways, for their purposes! He could be anywhere now, or dead for all she knew! *"Oh, Andy, Andy!"* she cried.

Dr. Atkinson, wide-eyed, asked, "How do you know about *Andy?"*

"Her son, she mean," Clarise said, patting Rosemary's hand. "His name's Andy too."

"Oh," Dr. Atkinson said, and took a breath. He leaned closer, patted Rosemary's hand and stroked her hair as she lay sobbing. "Miss—Mrs. Reilly," he said. "Rosemary . . . I know it's small comfort when you've lost so many years, but as far as I know, only two of the people who've been in such long comas have survived. That you've emerged, and emerged so—*cleanly*, in such relatively sound condition—well, it's a *miracle*, that's what it is, Rosemary, an absolute miracle."

2

They left her alone for a while, after Clarise had wiped her face with a damp cloth and smoothed her hair, and she had sipped down some water. She had asked for the back of the bed to be raised partway. She leaned against the pillow, looking out a window beyond the IV stand, at November trees fittingly bereft of leaves.

She had asked for a mirror too.

Not a good move.

She debated—then lifted the plastic handle from the blanket and took yet another wincing look at Aunt Peg wincing back at her. Weird, the likeness. The main difference was that darlin' Aunt Peg had been around fifty the last time Rosemary had seen her, whereas she herself was fifty-eight plus.

She had done 31 + 27 in her head twice, and got 58 both times.

And Andy was thirty-three.

The tears started again. She exchanged the mirror for the clump of moist tissue, blotted both eyes. *Get a grip on yourself, old lady. If he's alive he still needs you.*

They wouldn't have harmed him physically, of course; they worshiped him. That was the trouble. Being raised by Minnie and Roman Castevet & Company, not to mention the frequent adoring visitors from all over the globe, Andy must have grown up as spoiled and overindulged as the worst of the Roman emperors. And maybe as evil as—as she hated to think who. The coven must have done everything in their power to open and encourage that darker side of him.

She had worked against them, hoping to teach him love by loving him, honesty and responsibility by good example—the enlightened Summerhill creed. Even when he was too young to understand, she had taken him on her lap each evening before—

"Mrs. Reilly?"

She turned her head toward the doorway. An attractive, dark-haired woman leaned in, about her own age—her age *before*. The woman's navy suit, smart looking and not very futuristic, had white piping around its peaked lapels and an I ♥ ANDY button on one. Smiling, she said, "I'm Tara Seitz, the counselor here. If you'd rather be alone, I'll be on my way, but I've talked with other coma survivors; I think I can be a help to you. Can I come in?"

Rosemary nodded. "Yes," she said. "It's Miss, not Mrs. I'm divorced."

Tara Seitz came in and sat in the bedside chair, wafting Chanel No. 5. That, at least, was the same; Rosemary drew in a deeper breath of it.

Tara Seitz smiled a model's dimpled smile. "Dr. Atkinson is thrilled with how you're doing, Rosemary," she said. "He and Dr. Bandhu, our chief of staff, want to do some tests later; if the results are what Dr. Atkinson expects, you'll be able to start physical therapy tomorrow morning. The sooner you do start, the quicker you'll be out of here. We have a really great therapy team."

Rosemary said, "How soon do you . . ."

Tara, a palm raised, smiled and said, "That's not my department. My main message, I'm sorry to tell you, is that however distressed and disoriented you may be feeling now, tomorrow you'll be feeling even worse, much more aware of the time you lost. That's the way it is with shorter comas, and I'm sure yours wasn't basically any different."

Don't count on it, Tara. But she went on listening.

"But the day *after* tomorrow," Tara said, "you'll be feeling *better* than you do today, guaranteed, and better the day after, and so on. Try to remember that tomorrow. It'll be the pits, but it's all uphill from there. Truly."

Rosemary said, "I'll remember," and smiled at her. "Thanks."

"You have a son?" Tara asked.

"*Yes*," Rosemary said, and shook her head, sighing. "Thirty-three now. He could be *anywhere*. We had no family in New York, only—neighbors."

"No problem," Tara said. "We subscribe to a locator service." From a side pocket she drew what looked like a square black compact. Lifting its lid, she said, "What's his full name?"

Wonderingly, Rosemary said, "Andrew John Wood-house . . ."

Tara's dark eyes fixed on her.

"What's wrong?" she asked.

"You said Reilly," Tara said.

"That's my maiden name," Rosemary said. "My married name was Woodhouse."

"Oh," Tara said. The compact seemed to be a 1999 memo pad; she tattooed inside it with a stinger-pointed red fingernail, saying, "Andrew, John, Woodhouse. Spelled like it sounds?"

"Yes," Rosemary said. The fingernail seemed to have been groomed for its task; the others were filed short. Weird. "Date of birth?" Tara asked.

Rosemary almost said 6/66, the way the Castevets always did. "June twenty-fifth, 1966," she said.

Tara tattooed, closed the gizmo, and smiled her dimpled smile. "I'll enter the request pronto," she said. "We'll have a fix on him by five."

"*Five o'clock today?*" Rosemary said.

Tara shrugged, pocketing the thing. "Credit cards, school and car registrations, video rentals, book clubs," she said, "they're all on computers now, and the computers are all connected or can be gotten into one way or another."

"That's *wonderful!*" Rosemary said.

"It has its down side," Tara said, standing up. "Everybody's kvetching about loss of privacy. Would you like to watch TV? It's the best way I can think of for you to get caught up on things. You're going to see enormous changes." She opened the nightstand drawer. "For one thing," she said, "the Cold War is over. We won, they caved." She took out a slim brown paddle, pointed it across the room. "Oh, that dinky screen. They switched you in here last month; now I know why."

Moored to the wall above the dresser, a giant TV screen bloomed into color and music.

"I'll have maintenance give you a big one pronto," Tara said. "This is the remote. Have you worked one?"

"One *like* it," Rosemary said, taking the button-studded paddle. "Clunkier."

Tara bent over, tiding Chanel. "It's a snap," she said, pointing that stinger-tipped nail. "Volume up and down, channels up and down. These are for the color."

Rosemary thumbed the TV picture from a happy woman holding a can of beans to a happy baby eating cereal to a somber newscaster with an I ♥ ANDY button on his jacket. She froze her thumb. The mustached Negro newscaster talked about wild-fires in California.

"This is an all-news channel," Tara whispered in her ear. "It would be a good one to watch."

Rosemary, turning to her, asked, "Who's *Andy*?"

Tara stood up straight, drew in breath, and blew it out, pop-eyed. "Where to *begin*," she said—and gazed moonily at Rosemary. "*Andy*," she said, "is only the most beautiful, the most charismatic man on the face of the earth. He came out of no-where a few years ago—well, out of New York but nobody knew him before—and he's inspired and united the entire world. I don't mean united politically, I mean in terms of—fellow feeling and willingness to cooperate and respect each other. We were in really bad shape, believe me, with all the crazies coming out of the woodwork for the year 2000, and gunfire in the streets and all. Andy made us like realize that whether we call Him God or Allah or Buddha, we're all children of the *same one God*. He's shepherding us into the year 2000—Andy, I mean—as one hu-manity, refreshed and renewed."

Rosemary, leaning against the pillow, looking at her, said, "That's wonderful . . ."

Tara sighed, smiling at her, and said, "You'll see him any minute, guaranteed. GC runs a ton of commercials, all over the world, every language. That's his organization, foundation—both, I think. I saw him live last June at Radio City Music Hall. Talk about mesmerizing! He doesn't do many live appearances; mostly it's TV specials. And he spends a *lot* of his time alone, meditating. He's a very spiritual person but he's got this fun, human side too. He's just the greatest, *everybody* thinks so the buttons are in every language now even Braille!" She stopped for breath.

Rosemary said, "What's—his full name?"

"Adrian Steven Castevet," Tara said, "but he likes to be called Andy, by everybody."

Rosemary stayed looking at her.

Tara nodded. "Whether it's in a homeless shelter or a joint session of Congress," she said. "No difference. That's the kind of person he is. The first time he met *there he is! Look!*"

Rosemary turned.

Jesus!

The paddle slipped from her fingers as she stared.

He looked like *Jesus*—the calendar Jesus, not the hook-nosed Semite she had seen in NYU lecture slides. His longish hair and trim beard were tawny, his eyes hazel. His nose was straight, his jaw square.

Hazel eyes? Andy?

Where were his beautiful tiger eyes that had searched her own eyes so intently?

He was wearing contact lenses—or he'd had some kind of operation that had been developed while she was out. Nothing could mask him from her though, not the hazel eyes, not the beard, not the twenty-seven years. Andy. Andy. Andy.

"Oh foo, it's the short version," Tara said, as a golden sunlike symbol with GC in it appeared against a sky-blue background. "Isn't he a gorgeous person? Isn't he really someone special?"

Rosemary nodded.

"Keep watching," Tara said. "You'll see the long version. Other ones too. They're the best commercials on TV. Famous directors make them."

Rosemary took the paddle in her hand and looked at it as if she'd forgotten its purpose.

Tara said, "Are you all right?"

Rosemary looked at her, and asked, "What does GC stand for?"

Tara smiled at her. "God's Children," she said. "I'll be back later." She turned and headed for the doorway, and turned, pointing her stinger at Rosemary. "We're going to find you *your* Andy," she said. "Guaranteed!"

She saw the long version of the same commercial and two different short ones in the next five minutes.

Saw Andy at a distance, being applauded by an endless carpet of people in Central Park.

On the deck of an aircraft carrier, blocks of sailors cheering.

She saw Andy close up, looking her straight in the eye, warmly, lovingly, and a little playfully too. God, he had grown up handsome, the ordinary eyes notwithstanding. And she was being *objective* about it, not just his mother.

She heard him now, his voice strong but gentle, with the same sandy, sort of, texture that had been there yesterday when he was six. He didn't ask her to make a big *thing* about it, he just wanted her to give a little thought to the fact that we all really *are* descended from the same relatively small group of ancestors, whatever size, shape, and color they happened to be, and we really are all family. Did it make sense for us to be giving each other such bad times so often? Couldn't we all lighten up just a *little*, and light our candles, and so on . . .

She weighed it as she was lifted by Clarise and another nurse onto a gurney.

As she was wheeled into an examining room.

As Drs. Bandhu and Atkinson drew blood from her arm and passed electronic sensors over her limbs.

Either she had done a really super job of mothering during

Andy's early years—or the coven had found a really super disguise for the son of Satan.

That's who he was, there was no more trying to look the other way. He was Satan's son too, not just hers.

But wouldn't the coven, all its thirteen members, be dead by now? Even the youngest ones, Helen Wees and Stan Shand, had been in their sixties.

Whatever Andy was doing with a foundation called God's Children and its flood of commercials, it was *his* doing, not the coven's. He liked to be called Andy; wasn't that a good sign? From the very beginning, Roman had wanted to call him Adrian Steven—his father's name and his own real one—but she had vetoed it.

They'd had twenty-seven years to call him Adrian Steven or anything else they wanted. But he chose Andy.

Maybe *Summerhill* had worked.

She was sitting up in bed free of the IV, feeding herself soup, paused at one of the *dozens* of channels—the wife of a convicted murderer being interviewed by an unctuous jerk—when Tara came in hugging giant explosions of red roses and yellow and rust chrysanthemums. "Hi, look at you!" she said, carrying the bouquets to the dresser, berthing them there. "Nothing on your son yet, I'm sorry to say. They found forty-two Andrew John Woodhouses so far, but only one, in Aberdeen, Scotland, is the right age. He's a triplet. I'm sure they'll find yours."

Don't count on it, Tara. "All these interview programs," she said; "when I'm in decent shape, do you think I could get on one?"

Turning wide-eyed, Tara said, "Are you kidding? *These*— are from *them*! This one you're watching now, the roses, and his archenemy the mums. Somebody called somebody, who called somebody, who et cetera. Even as we speak, Channel Five is setting up across from the driveway."

Rosemary peered at her.

"You're famous!" Tara said. "Haven't you caught the news? You're the woman who came out of a twenty-seven-and-a-half-year coma this morning, and is now sitting up watching TV! And eating soup. You're going to be in the *Guinness Book of Records*. Did they have that back then?"

Rosemary nodded.

"When you're ready," Tara said, "you can be on any program you want to be on."

"Good," Rosemary said. "And I have sisters and brothers who should still be living, probably in Omaha; would you get your locator service after them?"

"Maybe they'll know where your son is," Tara said, coming to the bed with her memo gizmo in hand.

"I doubt it," Rosemary said.

"How about his father?"

She stayed silent a moment, then said, "Is there a famous actor named Guy Woodhouse? Stage and screen?"

Tara shook her head. "No," she said.

"Did you ever *hear* of a Guy Woodhouse?"

"Never," Tara said, "and I see *everything*."

"Then he's probably dead," Rosemary said.

Tara peered at her.

Rosemary gave her Brian's name and date of birth first, and then the others'.

Guy must have died early in the twenty-seven years.

Or Satan was a welsher—and why not? To mangle Oscar Wilde or whoever, once you commit rape, the next thing you know, you're not paying your debts.

For whichever reason, Guy hadn't gotten his agreed-upon price for nine months' use of her. He hadn't become the next Olivier or Brando.

Poor Guy.

Sorry, no more tears.

3

On Tuesday evening, November 23, two days before Thanksgiving and two weeks after her miraculous awakening, Rip Van Rosie—the tabloids' consensus—gave her first interview, live, on television.

With her hair refurbished (compliments of the hot new hairdresser), wrapped in a stylish coat (compliments of a leading department store), she stepped from the long white limo (compliments of the network) that had carried her to the West Side studio from the Waldorf-Astoria, where that morning she had checked into a tower suite (compliments of the management). Bracketed by security men, she walked ably and bravely through a rudeness of reporters.

"I was a production assistant at CBS-TV before I got married," she told the makeup woman prepping her.

"I heard that somewhere," the makeup woman said, powdering.

"In the sixties, women stayed home after," Rosemary said. "At least I did."

"I could live with that," the makeup woman said, brushing.

Enthroned in a tall chair, her dress (compliments of a leading bridal salon) caped with a towel (compliments of the makeup woman), Rosemary couldn't help but admire Aunt Peg in the mirror. Forty-five, tops. "You're a magician," she said.

"You've got good bones," the makeup woman said, spraying.

"What's left of them," Rosemary said.

She had chosen this program for two reasons: first, because it was broadcast live, so what she planned to say couldn't be edited out—in case, surprise, they thought she was crazy; and second, because the host seemed intelligent and genuinely interested in his guests.

She faced him across his narrow console, cameras lurking.

"Tell us, Rosemary," he said, leaning forward over his folded arms, "what was your very first thought when you came to?" He wore his customary shirtsleeves, suspenders, and I ♥ ANDY button.

Rosemary smiled. Home free. "My first thought was of my son Andy," she said.

"Yes, I know you had or have a son somewhere named Andrew. So you're really wearing your button for *two* Andys, right?"

She took a breath—*bless the man*—and smiled down at her I ♥ ANDY button. "No," she said, touching it, and looked up. "I'm wearing it for just one Andy—my son, Andrew John Woodhouse. We lived next door to people named Castevet, they were friends of ours. What happened, apparently, is after I went into the coma, they took care of Andy. Maybe they adopted him legally. I hope I'll be able to find out soon, now that I'm on my feet."

The host stared through his glasses at her. He said, "You're saying, Rip—Rosemary, that *Andy*, Andy Castevet, is *your son?*"

"Yes," she said. "I know Minnie Castevet is supposed to have been his mother, but she was much too old. Our apartment, Andy's and mine, was back to back with the Castevets'. That was in the Bram, the Bramford." Her face remained on the studio monitors, the camera poring over her mouth, her eyes.

"And . . . was Roman Castevet Andy's father?"

"No," she said. "Andy's father was my ex-husband, a man named Guy Woodhouse. I think he's dead now."

The host, blinking behind his glasses, said, "That's a stunning announcement, Rosemary Reilly. It's common knowledge, you know, that the Bram was Andy's boyhood home."

Rosemary said, "No, I didn't know that. That it's common knowledge, I mean."

"Have you tried to contact him?"

"That's what I'm doing now," she said. "I thought it would be a way to save a lot of explaining, to a lot of people who would all be skeptical."

"We'll find out," the host said, smiling at her across the console. "Maybe we'll be hearing from Andy before the end of the program." He turned to the camera, looking skeptical. "You never know," he said, close up. "We've had a presidential candidacy announced here, an embezzler arrested—why not Andy's real mother? We're going to take a break now; we'll be back with Rosemary Reilly, 'Rip Van Rosie,' and we'll have clips from Andy's appearances here plus your phone calls—and maybe a reaction from Andy himself. You *know* you're not going to touch that button!"

Telephone companies all over the world registered their highest ever three-minute surge in usage.

After two more breaks, the host leaned forward, shoulders hunched, and said, "Rosemary, during the last break we received a call from Diane Kalem, GC's press coordinator, who's also been a guest on this program. Andy is in his retreat in Arizona, but he's been told about the claim you've made here tonight, that you're in fact his mother. He's been watching for the past quarter hour." He glanced at the red-lighted camera—"Yo, Andy"—and looked back at Rosemary. "Diane tells me," he said, "and it comes as no surprise, that Andy wishes you well with all his heart, and he joins *everybody* in congratulating you on your miraculous recovery."

Rosemary said, "Thank you, I thank him." She glanced at the red-lighted camera.

"Diane also tells me that Andy has a question for you. Will you try to answer it?"

"Of course," Rosemary said.

"Andy would like to know," the host said, as the camera zoomed in for a close-up of him, "if you remember exactly what you were doing when you fell into your twenty-seven-and-a-half-year coma."

Cut to Rosemary. "Yes, I do," she said. "In my memory it was just two weeks ago. I was sitting at a desk by my bedroom window, an antique school desk with a top that lifts. I was typing a letter on an Olivetti portable." She turned to the red-lighted camera. "Andy was lying on the floor on his stomach," she said. "Watching television. *Kukla, Fran, and Ollie.*"

The host, across the console from her, chuckled as she faced him. "*Kukla, Fran, and Ollie* . . ." He turned to the camera, shaking his head, smiling. "It has the ring of truth to *me*," he said. "We'll wait to hear Andy's reaction. You never know what's coming next here. *Malmö, Sweden, you're on!*"

Andy asked for privacy, so another break was taken and Rosemary was shown into someone's empty office, where the phone on the desk blinked red.

She sat down, took a deep breath, and lifted the handset. Put it to her ear. Said, "Andy?"

"Tears are running down my face."

Her tears welled.

"They told me you *died*! I'm so angry—and so *joyful*, all in one moment—!"

Neither spoke.

She tried a desk drawer—locked—and another, looking for tissues.

"You there?"

Wiping with the side of her hand beneath her eyes, she said, "Yes, dear!"

"Listen. My press coordinator is on another line with them. You don't have to do the last segment if you don't want to. Do you?"

She weighed it, wiping. "I'll do it," she said. "He brought us together; I don't want to leave him stuck out there alone."

He laughed in her ear. What a laugh. "I forgot how sweet you are. No, no, I didn't forget. I'll talk too. We'll have to do a full press conference tomorrow, unless you don't want to. Where did they put you?"

"The Waldorf," she said. "This is *weird*! I'm talking with

a grown man and it's you! You were six two weeks ago, Andy!"

"When will you be there, *Mother?*"

"As soon as the program's over!" she said. "As soon as I can get there!"

"Figure on ten-thirty with traffic. I'll be there at ten-forty-five."

She gaped. "From *Arizona?*"

"I'm at Columbus Circle. I have an apartment here, over the GCNY offices. We'll say I'm flying in. What's your room number?"

"I can't remember! It's a tower suite!"

"I'll be there. You're gorgeous on television!"

Laughing-crying, she said, "Oh my angel, so are you!"

4

THE CROWD outside the studio, expanding exponentially, was excuse enough for a quick getaway. Rosemary repeated Andy's and her on-air promise to return to the program together, and went with the security men out a side door, through the kitchen of a Greek restaurant and a garage, to the limo waiting on Ninth Avenue—the escape route originally planned for just plain Rip Van Rosie.

The driver, a champ, had her back at the Waldorf by ten after. The security men steered her through the buzzing lobby into the right elevator and up to the right floor, the thirty-first. A concierge ran a card through the door lock for her as she signed scraps of paper from the security men's wallets.

The message gizmo by the foyer phone read 37. She pushed HOLD and DON'T RING.

By twenty of eleven she had showered, touched up the well-disguised old face—it still really sickened her—and was standing before the bedroom mirror pinning her I ♥ ANDY button to the least bizarre at-home garment among the mountains of stuff the stores had sent, a cobalt-blue velour caftan. Sort of.

A knock at the outer door stopped her heart. "*Room service!*" restarted it—she had ordered platters of shrimp and cheese. A white-haired waiter wheeled a table alongside the doorway, his face almost as red as his gilt-buttoned, I ♥ ANDY–buttoned jacket. "In the living room, ma'am?" he asked.

"Yes, please," she said, and followed after him and his dozen-domed table. "I only ordered shrimp and cheese."

"Compliments of the management, ma'am. Shall I open the bar?"

"Please," she said.

She turned the mammoth TV on while the waiter sprang table wings and rearranged domed dishes, silverware, napkins. The news was into sports already; she turned the thing off. "Isn't there a bill I can sign for the tip?" she asked.

"No, ma'am, most certainly not." He unfolded teak screens from a small mirrored bar. "I'd be honored, however . . ."

She signed a cocktail napkin for him.

She stood looking down through parted draperies at white and red lanes of car lights far below, lanes reaching up Park Avenue's separate sides and coming together blocks and blocks away. What would she say after the hugs and kisses? How would she frame the questions she had to ask? And more importantly, how could she be sure of the truth of Andy's answers?

It was fine calling him her angel, it was how she felt and it was good for his self-esteem. She had done it often, and often he had been angelic. But he was her half-devil too; she shouldn't let herself forget it, especially not tonight.

He had lied to her before, believably, and more than once. Just a few months ago—make that almost twenty-eight years ago—he had broken a small piece off Minnie and Roman's marble mantel, and totally convinced the three of them not only that he—a knock at the door.

She turned, starting toward the foyer, but *"Room service!"* came in, another red-jacketed waiter, shouldering a wine cooler and glasses on a tray. "Champagne, compliments of the management."

Stopping, sighing, she said, "Thanks, that's great. Would you put it on the bar please?" She returned to the window.

Five-and-a-half-year-old Andy had totally convinced all three of them not only—"Do I at least get a hug before I open it?"

She spun.

He stood by the bar beaming at her—Andy!— Jesus-handsome, combing his hair back with both hands, his bearded face flushed, his eyes shining. "I didn't want to attract attention," he said, coming toward her in his gilt-buttoned, I ♥ ANDY–buttoned red jacket, springing one side of his black bow tie, undoing his shirt collar, opening his arms.

After the hugs and kisses, the sighs and caresses and tears and tissues, he wrapped the champagne in a napkin, uncaged the cork and popped it—all with the panache of a union member.

Giggling, she said, "Where did you *get* all this stuff?"

"Downstairs in the bar," he said, laughing with her. "I swore a waiter to secrecy. You have no idea how glad everyone is to help me!" He tipped the wrapped bottle, pouring foam into her crystal tulip. Filled it to the brim . . .

Filled his own . . .

They gazed at each other over the glasses, he taller than she, as the foam fizzed down into pale gold wine. He shook his head. "Words can't say it," he said to her. Eyes locked, they clinked glasses, sipped.

"Contacts?" she asked him.

"Old-fashioned black magic," he said.

"They're beautiful," she said. "It's a real improvement."

Chuckling, he leaned and kissed her cheek. "And here I thought you were honest," he said. "Let's sit down, Mom. There's a lot I have to explain to you."

"**G**od's Children," Andy said, "was meant to be a trap, a deathtrap, a way to wipe out all human life. He was finally going to win. Instant Armageddon." His eyes blazed—so intensely she could almost see his tiger eyes again. "*Now,*" he said, "when I learn about *this,* that he *let them do it to you and never gave me a CLUE about it*—!" He drew in a long, deep breath. "Now, more than ever, I'm glad I fucked him! Excuse the language but that's what I did, Mom. I screwed up his Master Plan, thirty-three years in the making."

They sat close together, facing each other, clasping hands, on a dark cloud of sofa, each with a leg tucked under.

"It was why he came up when he did," he told her. "Covens are always 'summoning' him—real witches, fakes, fakes who think they're real, the whole range. He laughs. But he needed a child here who would be the right age by the year 2000. So when the Bramford coven called in '65, with you on the altar, he answered." She looked away. "I'm sorry," he said, bending, kissing her hands. "That was really brilliant of me. I'm sorry. It must have been an awful experience."

She drew breath. Looked at him. Said, "Go on. How was the plan supposed to work?" She watched him as he took a sip of champagne.

"Well," he said, licking his lips, setting the glass back on the coffee table, "first of all, there would be a charismatic leader, a great communicator." He smiled at her. "With normal-looking

human eyes. He would be the age Jesus was during *his* minis-
try; he might even brush up the resemblance a little." Lifting
his bearded chin, he brushed fingers beneath it. "Enough to
lure the Christians," he said, smiling, "not enough to scare the
Muslims and Buddhists and Jews. Being who he was, he'd have
the connections and funds to launch the best and biggest media
campaign in world history." He stopped smiling. Looked away.
Drew a troubled breath.

She watched him.

He looked back at her. "When it peaked," he said, "when
everyone on Earth trusted him except a handful of PA's—paranoid atheists—he would betray them. The best and biggest
betrayal in world history. Biochemicals. You don't want to
know."

She winced; biochemicals *sounded* deadly, whatever
they were.

He leaned closer to her, squeezing her hands. "That's
what I was bred for, Mother," he said. "By him and by the
coven. But when the strong members died—Minnie and
Roman and Abe—I began to ask questions. I was in my teens
then. A lot of the rites and rituals were laughable, and a lot
were—repulsive. I *like* humans, most of them, no matter *who*
created them; I'm half one, aren't I? Half you? *More* then half,
look at me!"

She nodded, biting her lip.

"So I rebelled," he said. "Your half of me got stronger than
his. Those few years we did have together"—he shook his head,
his eyes wet—"I tried so hard to keep the memory, the warmth
and sweetness, the *goodness* of you . . ." He knuckled an eye,
trying to smile at her.

Caressing his cheek, she said, "Ah my Andy . . ."

They leaned to each other, pecked lips.

She backhanded her cheek, smiling at him, blinking.

He shifted, loosed gilt buttons at his waist. "So as I said," he said, "I rebelled. He has no control over me while I'm here—more proof that my human side is stronger—so I decided to make GC into what *he* meant it only to *look* like, something *good* for humanity. Andy's message is simple and true and it doesn't turn anyone off except the PA's, and you know what, Mom? It works. The temperature's gone down a few degrees. Everybody's a little less short-tempered. Teachers and students, bosses and employees, husbands and wives, friends, *countries*—all going a little easier on each other. In a way, it's a tribute to you, Mom. Not in a way, that's what it is: a tribute to everything you gave me in those first few years."

She studied him. Said, "How does . . ."

"*He* feel?" He sighed, smiled. "How can I convey it? Picture a conservative father whose son joined the Peace Corps, then multiply it by ten."

She smiled at him, and said, "You know how to press a liberal's buttons."

"I'm a great communicator," he said, smiling back at her. "He's furious. We're on the outs. But while I'm here he can't do anything to stop me. If he could, he would have by now." He glanced at his watch, multidialed, black and gold. "I have to go," he said, getting up.

"So *soon*?" she said, getting up too, brushing his hand from her elbow.

"I've got visiting dignitaries," he said.

"You didn't *eat* anything! There's all this *food*!"

He reached into his jacket, chuckling. "*Mother*," he said, "from tomorrow on, you're not going to be able to get me out of your hair." Putting a card on the coffee table, he said, "The written number always reaches me, in minutes." He put his arm around her; they started toward the door. "There's a first-rate hotel in the lower floors of the building I'm in. We'll move you over there tomorrow morning. I'm in the penthouse—the fifty-second story, overlooking the park. You can't imagine the view. GCNY has three floors, the eighth, ninth, and tenth." In the foyer, he buttoned his shirt collar. "Do you think you'll be up to a press conference tomorrow afternoon? It would help if I knew now."

"Sure I will," she said, fastening the clip of his bow tie for him. "It'll be fun." His bearded chin high, he said, "I need the tray and the cooler. Otherwise I'm going to be spotted."

She held the door open a few inches with her slippered foot, watching him go to the bar; smiled at him as he returned. She said, "What a great Thanksgiving it's going to be!"

"Oh *shit*, I forgot," he said. "I'm committed. I have to go to Mike Van Buren's. Will you be my date? Please?" He stood before her, the tray at his shoulder. "I've *got* to go," he said. "Half the Republican right wing is going to be there. I slept over at the White House Saturday night and it's important I stay even-handed, with the primaries beginning."

"Well, it's not exactly my crowd," she said, buttoning his jacket for him, "but of course, my darling."

"They're going to flip over you," he said, smiling at her.

She stepped closer, looking up into his eyes. "Andy," she asked him, holding on to one of his gilt buttons, "have you been totally honest with me?"

His hazel eyes—which were *nice*, now that she was getting used to them—gazed earnestly, unswervingly into hers. "I swear I have, Mom," he said. "I know I lied when I was little. And I do now—plenty. But never again to you, Mom. Never. I owe you too much, I love you too much. Believe me."

Caressing his cheek, she said, "I do, my—baby."

"Oh *please*," he said.

They pecked, and she watched him go out with the cooler on his shoulder.

She closed the door, frowning.

5

ANDY'S MOM is at the Waldorf and you can bet Andy's there too—he jetted in from Arizona last night, it was on the news.

And there's going to be a press conference at GCNY headquarters at three this afternoon. That's at Columbus Circle.

Residents of the tristate area added together the available information, factored in a large sunny H extending over the entire region plus a four-day holiday starting tomorrow, and got into their cars, buses, Amtraks, LIRR's, B trains, D trains, rollerblades and strollers, and out of their midtown offices. By eleven o'clock, people of all sizes and descriptions packed every square foot of sidewalk on the logical route between point A and point B—nine blocks north on Park Avenue, and five blocks west, three of them double-length, on East Fifty-ninth Street and Central Park South.

Members of the NYPD, already burdened with preparations for the Thanksgiving Day parade, might well have been expected to show a degree of surliness as they braced themselves against creaking barriers—but smiles and good spirits prevailed. Wasn't this all for *Andy*? And Andy's *Mom*, for chrissake?

In the foyer of the suite, Andy and Rosemary hugged each other, he in a GC zipper jacket, jeans, and sneakers, she in a designer suit, her I ♥ ANDY button, and heels. He presented the group he had brought with him—his press coordinator Diane, his buddy and driver Joe, a secretary, Judy, who would get those 429 messages transferred to GC's computer and prioritized, and Muhammed and Kevin, already in the bedroom assembling corrugated cartons for her clothes. They had driven over in an unmarked van, through the park at Sixty-fifth Street and down Second Avenue, to avoid the crowds. "Have you seen what's going on out there?" Diane asked.

"I can't believe it!" Rosemary said. "It's like when the Pope was here, and President Kennedy!"

Diane nodded. Her feathered hair was gray, her eyes violet; she was late-sixtyish. A gold GC logo hung on the bosom of her dark queen-size dress. "All those patient people," she said in a diva's deep contralto, "waiting and praying for a glimpse of the mother of your son! From what I saw last night, I knew you wouldn't want to fly past them in a limousine with tinted windows; you're a gracious, warm-hearted woman. So I took it upon myself"—she clapped a hand to her bosom, sending velveteen shock waves—"Andy had nothing to do with it, it was *my* idea, but he's agreeable if you are . . ."

Reclining side by side on patched fake-leather upholstery, their hands—his right, her left—meshed between them, they clip-clopped up Park Avenue in a horse-drawn open carriage, waving and smiling and nodding at the barrier-bound crowds clapping on both sides, at the homemade I ♥ ANDY and I ♥ Andy's Mom signs, at the hands waving from office-building windows.

A rolling police car led the way; security men walked alongside; another sat high in front with the top-hatted driver. Every

block or so, Andy hugged Rosemary and kissed her cheek; the
crowd cheered. He leaned to speak in her ear—"Makes you feel
like an idiot after a while, doesn't it?"—and the crowd cheered
louder.

News choppers whanged away at the sky. When the slow
procession below took its westward turn at Fifty-ninth Street—
police car, horse-and-carriage, police car—Park Avenue's left
lanes were cobbled with cars all the way up through the Sixties
and Seventies.

They had to wait a few minutes at Fifth Avenue till cameras stopped rolling in front of the floodlit Plaza Hotel. He said
in her ear, "Movies, commercials, fashion shoots, you can't get
anywhere in this town." The crowd cheered.

They clip-clopped along Central Park South, waving, smiling, nodding at even bigger crowds, more signs—I ♥ ANDY,
I ♥ ROSEMARY—spreading into the park, climbing the trees.

Ahead, where the park ended, a glittering tower of golden
glass rammed high in the blue sky.

Shaking her head, Rosemary turned to Andy. "I'm dreaming,"
she said, and kissed his cheek and hugged him. The crowd roared.

Pointing ahead over the slim microphone, she said, "You."
          "Thank you. Which name do you want to be called
by—Reilly, Woodhouse, or Castevet?"

She said, "Well . . . everyone seems to go right to first names
now—I don't know if that's Andy's influence or if it would have
happened anyway"—a small laugh surprised her—"so just Rosemary will be fine," she said. "Legally, I'm Rosemary Eileen Reilly.
Actually I guess the name I like best is the one I saw today on
some of the signs, Andy's Mom."

Laughter, and a spatter of clapping, a sizzle of cameras. Diane, among the standees, clapped fortissimo, smiling and nodding.

The Tower had been an office building in an earlier incarnation, a motion-picture company's headquarters; its high ceilings had enabled GCNY's architect to design its auditorium, on the ninth floor, in the form of a semi-circular amphitheater—Andy's concept. Five steep steps, carpeted in forest green like every square inch of the place, held sixty or so people; another twenty stood at the sides. On the half-moon stage, Andy and Rosemary sat at a table draped with sky blue and hung with a gilded GC logo. A trio of black video cameras clung to ceiling rods, turning beaked heads this way and that, pausing, turning. Muhammed and Kevin roamed with fishpole mikes.

Rosemary, smiling as the clapping petered out, pointed to her left and said, "You. No, you. Yes."

"Rosemary, how do you feel about having missed out on Andy's whole growing up?"

"Awful," she said. "That's definitely the worst part of the experience. But I'm glad"—she smiled at Andy, squeezed his hand—"that he managed so well without me."

He leaned close. "I didn't," he said. "I didn't, and Mom didn't miss the whole thing. I told her last night—or early this morning, I should say—that she was with me during the most important years, one to six. She's the one who set my feet in the path I'm following today." He kissed her cheek.

Clapping. Cameras. "Rosemary!" "Rosemary!"

She pointed. "You."

"Rosemary, so far no one's been able to locate Andy's real father or find any information about him since the summer of 1966. Can you explain why that is?"

"No, I can't," she said. "Guy went out to California then, and we divorced and lost touch."

"Would you tell us more about him?"

She stayed silent. Cleared her throat. Said, "He was a very good actor, as I said last night. He was in three Broadway plays, *Luther, Nobody Loves an Albatross,* and *Gunpoint.* We had our differences, obviously, but he was, or is—a fine person, very— thoughtful, unselfish—"

"There are still areas," Andy said, his hand on her arm, "where Mom's memory hasn't fully returned. Please, could we have a different question? John?"

She wanted to speak to him alone, but when they got to her seventh-floor suite, the living room was occupied by a dozen men and women, the inner circle of GCNY. A waiter offered hors d'oeuvres, a bartender poured wine. Diane presented William-the-legal-director and Sandy-the-publications-director, and before Rosemary had even gotten on a last-name basis with them, still on her first Gibson, Andy was touching her shoulder with a sorry-gotta-go-now look in those really beautiful hazel eyes. He apologized to William and Sandy, drawing her aside.

"I'm sorry, Mom, I have to go now," he said. "Some public-health officials from Louisiana are coming to see me, it was set up last week and I'm not sure what it's about or how long it's going to take. If you need anything or want to see a show tonight, ask Diane, or Judy or Joe. Van Buren's farm is in Pennsylvania; we'll be driving, leaving at noon." He tipped his tawny head toward the window. "Joe'll call for you." He kissed her cheek and left.

Joe stood by the window some twenty feet away, holding a glass at his lips, looking at someone or something down in the park or just thinking—big and solid looking, in a tan corduroy jacket and jeans. Men seemed to be wearing jeans everywhere now. His hair was graying but he was oddly attractive for an old man—sexy in a way. She hadn't felt *that* in a while.

A *really* old man. Her age plus two. Maybe. He turned, saw her looking. She smiled. "Rosemary"—Diane clamped her shoulder, turning her—"Jay our financial director wants to meet you."

"Such an honor, Rosemary!" Jay said. "Such a blessing! And that ride! Diane, you're a genius!" He looked like a jay—small, beaky, bright-eyed behind glasses, with hair from the raven side of the family. "Over an hour's exposure, *global* exposure!" he crowed. "At a total cost of five hundred dollars! That's *if* the stable bills us, and chances are they won't!"

She excused herself and went to the bar for a refill.

"We don't get many calls for Gibsons nowadays," the bartender said, stirring.

"Andy's Mom?"

She turned. "Crab cakes," Joe said, holding out a pair of wood picks.

"Oh, thanks, Joe," she said, taking one.

He asked the bartender for a scotch, and they ate the hot round crab cakes, eye-smiling at each other. His eyes were dark brown; his nose looked as if it had survived a break or two.

"Good," she said.

"Mmm," he said, wiping his lips with a napkin, finishing chewing. "I can't tell you, Rosemary," he said, "how proud I am to know your son up close and to be able to help him. I thought my best years were behind me—I was a cop here in the city, gold badge—but was I ever wrong. And now that *you're* part of the picture too—well, I don't know what to say."

"How about cheers," she said, smiling.

"Good idea," he said.

"Cheers," they said, and clinked glasses and sipped.

No ring on his finger. Did that still mean anything? She rested her left hand on the bar.

"Anybody gives you any trouble," he said to her, "I'm the guy you want to speak to. Nuts or pests—and rest assured you'll be getting them—any problems of any kind whatsoever, just let me know."

"Will do," she said.

"When Andy's at the retreat," he said, "or just busy somewhere and doesn't need me, I usually hang out up in the spa on the fortieth floor. And I live right over on Ninth Avenue. So don't hesitate."

"I won't," she said. "What's your last name, Joe?"

He sighed. "Maffia," he said. Raised two fingers. "Two F's, and no, I don't belong, and yes, I get a lot of respect."

She smiled at him. "I'm sure you would if you were Joe Smith," she said.

"Rosemary," Diane said, clamping her shoulder, turning her around, "Craig is especially anxious to meet you. He's our director of TV production."

While she was talking with Craig, Joe touched a fingertip to her shoulder. "Take care," he said. "Andy said twelve noon."

She didn't want to offend Joe Maffia—because she liked him, not for what she imagined were the more common reasons—so for the first fifteen minutes or so it was a three-way conversation. He explained over his shoulder why the Vikings had a good chance of upsetting the Cowboys, and she told him and Andy about the temptation to drop sharp objects when viewing the Macy's balloons from a floor above, and about being screamed and waved at and having to do the whole Princess-Grace-on-the-balcony bit from the bedroom window.

When they got out of the Lincoln Tunnel, though, she signed to Andy, and in the next space of silence he put a finger into the armrest at his right. A wide black shield slid up from the back of the front seat, blocking out the balding back of Joe's head and half the daylight too, closing them in a humming black-leather roomette lit bluely through tinted glass.

"*Andy,*" she whispered, "*I'm so uncomfortable having to watch what I say about Guy, and the divorce, and—*"

"You handled it beautifully," he said. "It was just that one question."

"*And the ones about Minnie and Roman?*"

He shrugged. "Don't do any more interviews. If you don't enjoy them, there's no reason to. But really, you were fine. Here, look again. Read." He had the papers there. The front pages of both tabloids were the same full-page photo of him kissing her cheek at the press conference, one overlaid with a white GIVING THANKS!, the other with THANKSGIVING! "And you don't have to whisper," he said, nodding his head toward the front. "He listens to tapes or sports. He can't hear a thing from here; believe me, I know." He Groucho-Marxed his eyebrows.

"What about the others?" she asked. "I don't know who knows what—Diane, William—"

"Nobody knows anything!" he said.

"They aren't involved in . . .?"

"What? Witchcraft? Satanism?"

She gave a nod.

He laughed. "I promise you they're not," he said. "I had enough of that to last me a lifetime. Ten lifetimes. Everyone who works for GC—the key people, I mean—they were picked by me and hired by me *after I decided to change things around.*

William was our ambassador to Finland under three presidents. Diane is like the queen of press people; she was with the Theatre Guild for thirty-five years. They have no idea GC was ever intended to be anything but what it is—an organization that's helping people in lots of different ways. They're proud to be part of it, and the same goes for all the others."

She said, "But where do they think it *came* from?"

"The same place everyone else does," he said. "It was founded and endowed years ago by an anonymous group of high-minded industrialists. It's all documented. And as far as who my father is"—he took her hands, leaned closer—"there are now exactly two people on earth—which reminds me, there's something else I have to tell you, don't let me forget—there are now only two people on earth who know who he is." He swung a finger back and forth between them. "Us." He squeezed her hands, held her eyes with his. "That's why it's such—*joy* for me to be with you again. Not just because you're my mother. Because you *know who I am*, because I don't *have to hide the truth from you*! And don't you feel something like that toward me? How many people have you told about that night back then?"

Shaking her head, she said, "No one. Who would believe me?"

"I do," he said.

They looked at each other—hugged each other tight. "I love you so much!" he said in her ear, and she in his, "Oh Andy, I love *you*, darling!" They kissed each other's temples, kissed cheeks, the corners of their mouths—she pushed; they let each other go, turned.

Sat apart.

Breathing.

He fingered-combed his hair back, turned to the window, looked out. Touched the armrest; the window tops on both sides dropped half an inch.

She looked out her window at a shopping mall swinging past. Brown hills.

"Stan Shand died November ninth."

She turned.

"At the same time you woke up," he said, "just after eleven. A cab hit him in front of the Beacon Theater."

She winced, drew breath.

"It can't possibly be a coincidence," he said. "He was the last one alive of the coven, the thirteenth. Roman said there were spells that went on forever and spells that stopped when the last caster died. He left me one of his engravings, Stan; that's how I found out. He's the one who taught me art and music, and the right way to floss." He showed his teeth.

She smiled, sighed. "I wish he had died a few years sooner," she said.

"It wouldn't have helped you much. Leah Fountain only died a couple of months ago. She was over a hundred."

The leather roomette took a wide right turn.

"Andy, listen," Rosemary said. "Once I got going with the physical therapists, I conked out whenever I hit the pillow. Tuesday and yesterday were—*crazy*, and last night I was reading an almanac I got at the newsstand but I'm not up to date yet. Is Mike Van Buren the TV evangelist who's also the head of the Christian Consortium?"

"No, no," Andy said. "That's Rob Patterson. Mike Van Buren is the former TV commentator who's bolted the Republicans and is running as a third-party candidate."

"I hope I don't get them mixed up," Rosemary said.

6

MIKE VAN BUREN, in a red tie, white shirt, blue suit, and gold I ♥ ANDY button, a carving knife in one hand and a two-pronged fork in the other, stepped back from the head of the table to allow his sister and campaign manager Brooke, in a white apron over a blue dress, to set down a large, succulent turkey bedded in parsley on a white china platter. The guests clapped, twelve on each side of the table, their faces bright with light bouncing from white damask, white china, silver, and glass.

Brooke moved aside, shaking her hands and blowing at them, as Mike stepped forward. "It's just beautiful, Brooke!" he said. "Compliments to Dinah!"

Another hand for Dinah—in the kitchen, presumably, and not alone.

Rosemary, seated at Van Buren's left, scanned the opposite team as she clapped. Could you believe it? Every man, from Andy across from her down to Joe, and the men on her side of the table too—she leaned forward and looked past Rob

Patterson clapping—yes, every last man at the table had on a basically red tie, a white shirt, and a blue suit. All wore plain or fancy I ♥ ANDY buttons—except, of course, the Great Communicator himself. At least his suit had a pinstripe. And of course he looked fabulous, dressed decently for a change.

"Folks . . ." Van Buren said. He stood behind the turkey with his arms at his sides, waiting for silence. "Before we go any further . . ." He turned to his right and smiled. "Andy, will you do us the honor of saying grace?"

"No, sir," Andy said, smiling back at him, "not when Rob Patterson is at the table."

Murmurs of approval hummed. Mark Mead, the executive director of Patterson's Christian Consortium, leaned clear of the woman at his left and smiled at Andy. "Well spoken, Andy," he said.

Patterson himself, standing up beside Rosemary, said, "Thank you, Andy. I've never been more flattered in my life. If you'll bow your heads . . ."

Rosemary stole a peek across the table; Andy winked at her, and rubbed at his eye as if something had gotten into it.

When the relatively brief sermon was over, Van Buren started carving. He was good at it; you had to give him credit. Leaning over the turkey, operating on its outer side with knife, fork, and occasional shears, he sliced off leaf after unbroken leaf of dark meat and light, talking all the while. "As a former broadcaster myself, Rosemary, I can tell you with a fair degree of authority that you acquitted yourself magnificently yesterday."

"Thank you," she said.

"You radiate candor and sincerity. Those are admirable qualities in a woman."

"And not in a man?" she asked.

"And a ready wit!" Van Buren cast a pixie smile at her, slicing away. "That's something I value highly."

"Rosemary, my dear."

She turned to Rob Patterson.

"That was so gracious of Andy," he said. "So typical of his boundless generosity. It's a moment I'll treasure the rest of my life."

Smiling at him, she said, "You're too kind."

"Sometimes, Rosemary," Rob Patterson said, touching her wrist, "I feel that Andy himself is a mite too kind, and too generous, and too forbearing. I'm thinking in particular about PA's, in connection with the candles. I hope you don't share your son's tolerant position. I feel Mike is dead right on this one; something *has* to be done about them, they're going to spoil it for the rest of us!"

She knew that PA's were paranoid atheists, and one of the GC commercials she had seen early on had something to do with candles, but she had no idea what the man was talking about. She looked for help, but the Great Communicator was communicating with the Great Slicer.

The woman beyond Patterson rescued her, slapping his arm with gusto. "Now, Rob, don't you start bawling about PA's again! This is the day we count our blessings, not our curses, isn't that so, Rosemary? Andy says a few candles more or less won't matter a snip and that's good enough for me! Rosemary, you must be popping out of your skin with pride! Merle and I, we celebrate if the boys stay two years in the same school!"

"Andy," Mark Mead said, leaning clear of the woman on his left, smiling, "would you mind passing me the celery?"

Joe, down at the end of the table, caught her eye, waggled fingers at her.

She smiled, waggled back.

He too looked good in Republican, sitting there with his head on his hand listening to Mrs. Lush Rambeau.

"*YOW! JESUS!*" Van Buren dropped the knife and clutched his hand, red blood dripping on white turkey breast.

Gasping, Rosemary thrust her napkin at him.

As soon as Andy climbed into the back of the limo after her, she collapsed against his shoulder, moaning. "*Ye gods! What a—yuuch!* Yowwww!" He hugged her as their black roomette rolled forward. "Ah, poor baby," he said, raining kisses on her head, "thank you, thank you. The corn fritters were good, weren't they?"

She mumbled something in his coat, and squirmed her head around to look up at him. "Am I crazy," she asked, "or was the table set to look like the Norman Rockwell painting?"

He smacked his forehead. "*Yes!*" he said. "That's it! I kept feeling déjà vu! That's what it was! All the white stuff, and the plain glasses . . ."

"And Brooke's dress and apron, that's in the picture too I think."

They sighed. He let go of her and they sat up straight, shaking their heads. Settled their coats, fixed their hair.

Lights whipped by bluishly, a steady lashing.

"Hey, what is it with the candles?" she asked. "I saw something about them early on, but then . . ."

"A thing we're doing," he said. "Tell you later. You think Mark Mead is gay?"

"The possibility crossed my mind," she said.

"I think he was coming on to me."

"Van Buren was coming on to *me*," she said. "I radiate candor and sincerity."

"Well you *do*," he said, poking at her hair.

"Yeah," she said. "Especially when I'm lying to the entire world on TV."

"We said, no more interviews. Unless you want to."

"How about conversations with people?"

They looked out their windows. A slower lashing began, amber lights.

"You know why he was, don't you?"

"Why who was what?" she asked, turning.

"Why Van Buren was coming on to you," he said.

"I radiate candor and sincerity," she told him. "And I have a ready wit."

"And a charming innocence," he said. "You also radiate *signatures*. On petitions. One date with you and he's on the ballot in every state."

She leaned away, peering at him. "Go on with you," she said.

He smiled at her. "You've got *clout*, Ma!" he said. "People heart Andy's Mom even more than they heart Andy."

"Oh go *on*," she said, giving him a poke.

He chuckled.

She sat back. Settled herself against his shoulder.

Pink lights, slow and steady.

"What was Saturday night at the White House like?"

He told her for fifteen miles or so.

"Wow," she said.

He sighed. "Democrats are more fun," he said. "There's no getting around it."

"The only exits," he said, "are at the garage levels, the lobby, on eight, nine, and ten, and my apartment. It's the highest-speed elevator allowed by law; only six of them in the city. Two thousand feet per minute. That comes down to—" "Spare me the details," she said. They stood face to bearded chin in a cylindrical cab not much wider than a phone booth, rocketing upward faster, far faster, than she liked. The thing was like a lipstick turned inside out—red leather to shoulder height, her shoulders, and brass, or solid gold for all she knew, from there up to the glowing ceiling. "He put this in just for you?" "He owes me." They waggled their jaws till their ears popped. "I've scored a few times in here." "Spare me *those* details too, Andy." "Here we are. Brace yourself for the mother of all views, mother of all mothers." A red 52 pinged alight above his head as they slowed.

The cab split open behind him; he backed out through widening space, taking her hand, leading her out—his other hand slapping wall—into a softly lit, black-floored, art-movie-house-lounge kind of space, sparely but handsomely furnished in brass-trimmed black, its far wall a Cinerama of city and stars and three-quarter moon, moving lights of planes.

"Oh Andy!" she said, and gasped, biting her lip.

He led her forward, lifting her coat away, dropping it, shedding his own as they passed between sofas. She swayed—at an open plane door a good few minutes from touchdown. The park below was dark carpet lightly salted; the East Side and miles beyond, a glittering World's Fair display. The white moon above washed stars from the cobalt sky.

"A perfect night," he said behind her, harnessing her between his elbows, holding her shoulders from the front. She leaned back against him, sighed. "I ordered a full moon," he said, his cheek at her temple, "and they sent that. What are you gonna do?"

She smiled, scanning the glittering diorama, caressing his

hand on her shoulder. He reached his other arm out, pointing. "That's the Whitestone Bridge . . . And that's Queens, the whole shootin' match . . ."

"It's incredible," she said.

His arm dropped; he held her at waist and shoulder, kissed her ear. "*I* had a twenty-seven-year hole too," he said, his breath hot, "only I was awake through mine."

"Andy—"

"You weren't around when I learned about women, and in my teens and all, so now, at the same time we have this tremendous bond between us, you're someone who just came into my life—older, sure, but more beautiful than any other woman on this whole planet." He turned her around and mouthed her mouth, clamped her head and waist, rammed hard at her middle, tongued her tongue. She fought free; he drew back— tiger eyes fading to hazel—taking his arms, his hands from her, breathing hard.

She backhanded her mouth, staring at him, quivering, doubly shocked by what she had seen and what he had done to her.

She said, "Your old eyes . . ."

He drew breath, put a hand up for time out, swallowed. Drew breath. Looked at her, hazel-eyed. Nodded. "They're still there," he said. "It's a way of—willing them to look different. I lost control a little."

She stared at him. "A little?" she said. "That was 'losing control a *little*'?"

He leaned to her: "*You're the only woman, the only person, I can be myself with!*" His eyes tigered as he spoke, and faded.

He took a breath, stood straight, shook his head as if to clear it. "With everybody else," he said, "I'm afraid to let go all the way. Even in the dark."

She backed around him, shaking her head, a hand up. "I'm sorry, Andy," she said. "I feel for you, I *love* you, but—" She shook her head, backed away a few feet.

He raised both hands. "I'm the sorry one," he said. "I lost *a lot* of control, not a little. Never again. I swear. Please. Please forgive me. Listen, I was going to tell you. I'm going away tomorrow and maybe it's a good thing. It is. You can go visit your family. I'm going to the retreat for a few days and then I have to go to Rome and Madrid. I'll be back December sixth, that's a week from Monday."

She let breath out. Nodded. "I guess it is a good thing," she said. "Maybe we've both been—trying too hard to make up for lost time."

"Don't blame yourself," he said. "It was *me*, not we."

"Don't ever," she said, "*ever*, let anything like that happen again."

"I won't, I swear."

She drew a breath. "Good night," she said. "When are you going?"

"Early," he said. "Joe's driving me to the airport, but then he'll be around if you need him. Everybody else too. Whatever you want, just ask. And you've got the number I gave you; it works everywhere."

She said, "Thank you," and turned and picked up her coat. And turned again. "Have a good trip," she said.

He half-smiled. "You too. Do you think you'll go?"

"Probably," she said. Looked at him. "I love you," she said.

"I love *you*," he said. "Please, forgive me."

"How do I get to the regular elevator?" she asked.

"Take this one," he said. "You can get out at the lobby and then just go around to your right. You'll be at seven while you'd still be waiting."

Sighing, she said, "And seasick to boot"—but turned and went to the onyx wall, touched the button by the brass cylinder, splitting it open. She stepped into the Revlon Express, turned and waved at him before the glittering, flickering lights. He kissed at her.

She touched L, and as the cab closed around her, DOOR OPEN.

He had turned to the window; the light turned him back. He looked at her, brows up.

"The candles," she said. "You were going to tell me."

"Oh," he said. Smiled and shrugged. "It's just a thing we're doing, lighting candles, to welcome in the year 2000. Kind of a corny idea, but people went for it, except the PA's. Even most atheists are lighting them—what's the big deal?—but there's this handful, because our name is God's Children."

She stepped out of the cab, peering across the room at him. "You mean, *everybody's* lighting candles?" she asked. "Everybody in the whole country?"

"In the whole world," he said. "Except a few bushmen maybe. Out in the streets and parks, in homes, stores, schools, churches, mosques, synagogues, cathouses, you name it. In the exact same minute. The first minute of the year 2000, Greenwich Mean Time. Seven p.m. here, midnight in London, morning in Moscow . . . It's supposed to symbolize—you know, 'one humanity, refreshed and renewed.'"

She stared across the room at him, standing there before the moon and the stars and the city. "Andy," she said, "that's not *corny*, that's a *lovely* idea. . . ." She took a few steps toward him. "It'll be like a billion points of light!" The brass cylinder closed behind her.

Andy smiled. "More like *eight* billion," he said. "The candles are neat: sky blue on the outside, with a yellow core. So when you look down on them from the top, it's like the logo."

She said, "There are special candles?"

Nodding, he said, "In glasses." He showed juice-glass height with finger and thumb. "We've been making them for over a year now," he said. "It's one of our biggest projects. Fourteen factories in Japan and Korea. Working day and night, seven days a week."

"Oh, Andy!" she said, dropping her coat and going to him. "It's a *beautiful* idea! Who thought of it?"

He did a little aw-shucks shuffling, grinned at her. "Three guesses," he said.

She hugged him. "Oh my *angel!*" She kissed his cheek. "It's wonderful! It'll make New Year's Eve a *really significant happening* for the entire human race!"

"That's the general idea," he said, smiling at her.

"It's *glorious!*" She hugged and kissed him. "I'm so *proud* of you!" She hugged and kissed him. He said, "If you expect me to behave myself . . ."

"Oops!" Hands in the air, she backed off. Kissed at him, picked up her coat. "Have a wonderful, wonderful trip," she said. "Hurry home, darling! I'll miss you so!"

"Same here, Mom," he said, beaming at her before his universe of lights.

She pushed the button, got in the cab, turned and waved, touched L.

Heaved a sigh as the cab enclosed her.

What a beautiful, beautiful concept! Everyone, everywhere, all of civilized humanity, lighting sky-blue-and-yellow GC candles, in the year 2000's very first minute, Greenwich Mean Time!

Too bad a few cranks would be taking the edge off it, but they certainly had their rights, as Andy himself clearly knew.

What an angel! No wonder the whole world loved him!

Really: Had *any* mother, *any*where, *ever* had so much reason for pride in a son?

Only Mary, she answered herself—dropping two thousand feet a minute toward the center of the earth—*only Mary*.

TWO

7

SHE DECIDED to put off visiting Omaha till after New Year's. Of her five sisters and brothers, all older than she, three were alive, a sister and two brothers. She had spoken on the phone with each of them twice, once as Rip Van Rosie and once as Andy's Mom—which was probably one time more than she had spoken with them in the whole year before the coven zapped her. Brian, the one she loved best, who had joined AA, thank God, and been dry since '82, was leaving Monday with his wife, Dodie, on a thirty-fifth-anniversary 'round-the-world cruise—they'd be lighting their candles in Auckland, New Zealand—and Eddie, the one she loved least, sounded unchanged by time. "You tell Andy that his Uncle Ed speaks for thirty thousand union meat packers when he says, with all due respect, he should stop being such a softy about the PA's. Van Buren's right; we should *make* them light candles, at gunpoint if need be."

Judy was Vassar '93 and beautiful, with sleek black hair demurely bunned, cinnamon skin, lavishly black-rimmed eyes, and a dime-size red dot above the bridge of her nose. Her I ♥ ANDY button was pinned to pastel saris; her last name was Kharyat. On Monday morning, swathed in lime silk, she brought Rosemary a computer-printed breakdown of the thousands of messages that had come in as of six the evening before, along with suggested response formats that would cover almost all of them.

She sniffed and dabbed at her eyes every now and then while she and Rosemary worked at the table by the living room window. The mascara wasn't going to make it through lunch. Rosemary touched her hand and said, "Judy, is something wrong?"

Judy sighed, brown eyes looking woefully through their black mini-mask. "A *guy*," she said, and looked upward. "Listen to me! I can't believe it!" She sniffed, dabbed with her tissues.

Rosemary sighed and nodded, remembering her own Guy. "They sure can screw you up," she said. Patted Judy's hand. "If you want to talk," she said, "I'm a good listener." Dying to hear.

"Thanks," Judy said, mustering a smile, dabbing. "I'm surviving."

Rosemary spotted crossword-puzzle squares, neatly inked, in Judy's attaché case when she was getting ready to leave. "Do you play Scrabble?" she asked.

The beautiful Indian face lit up. "You bet! A two-minute time limit, blanks wild?"

"Um . . . One night real soon," Rosemary said.

The TV division occupied the northwest quarter of the tenth floor. Approaching Craig's corner office, Rosemary walked through a few thousand square feet of empty cubicles with barren desks—computers and phones, no people. Pictures and papers tacked to partitions . . .

Craig and Kevin, in GC T-shirts and jeans, sat with their sneakers up on a coffee table, watching TV—Edward G. Robinson in a black-and-white movie. They were black and white themselves (you were *supposed to* use black now, Negro was out). Craig looked like Adam Clayton Powell and Kevin looked like a nineteen-year-old kid named Kevin—except that today some nineteen-year-old Kevins were probably short and Chinese. "Rosemary! Hi!" they said, jumping to their feet. Kevin knocked over his Coke.

"Sit, sit," Rosemary said. "Wow, what a view!" She went to the window, looking out across West Side buildings at the Hudson River and the George Washington Bridge in its end-to-end entirety.

"Isn't it great?" Craig's deep voice asked behind her.

"Fantastic!" She turned, nodded toward the doorway. "Where is everybody?" she asked.

Craig said, "Vacation between Thanksgiving and New Year's. The whole shebang."

"*That's* generous," she said.

"That's Andy," he said, smiling. "There isn't much to do here; the New Year's Eve show is in the can."

"What about what's in the pipeline?" she asked.

"There isn't much," Craig said. "We're cutting back on production next year. Mostly reruns."

Kevin wiped the table with paper towels.

"What are you watching?" Rosemary asked, looking at Robinson pleading with Hedy Lamarr, no, the one who looked like her.

"*The Woman in the Window*," Craig said. "Fritz Lang, 1944."

"I don't think I've seen it," she said.

"It's good. Noir."

The three of them sat and watched a few minutes.

Craig said, "Is there anything in particular you wanted to see me about?"

"Yes, there is," Rosemary said.

"I'm sorry, I should have asked right away." He got up. "You go on watching," he said to Kevin, "we'll go inside."

He showed Rosemary into an office next door. Here it looked as if work were done; two desks were piled with papers and computer printouts and magazines, a wall was banked with monitors, speakers, and audio equipment, the other walls were shelves of cassettes and records. Craig cleared two castered chairs.

When Rosemary had seated herself, Craig sat, rolled his chair fairly close, and leaned forward, elbows on the chair arms, hands folded, his head cocked, ready to listen.

Rosemary said, "I worry that even though Andy has lowered the temperature all around, there's a hot spot where the PA's are concerned, and the way some people are reacting to them. I don't know what you have in the works—"

"Almost nothing," Craig said.

"—and I don't want to butt in where I'm not needed—"

"Rosemary," he said, "we would welcome any suggestions you care to offer."

She said, "I know Andy wants their rights to be respected, but doesn't it look as if he hasn't done enough about it? I'd like to see a commercial that addresses the issue head-on, and I mean head-on, where he's talking straight at my brother Eddie the gun collector, while there's still time to cool things down before New Year's. So it would have to be done quickly. But simple would be better than elaborate, I think."

Craig looked down, a sneakered foot tapping. He looked at her. "That makes a lot of sense, Rosemary," he said. "Have you spoken to Andy about it?"

"No," she said. "I wanted to check first and see if anything was in the works, and to sound *you* out."

"Thanks, I appreciate that," Craig said. "Hey, I've got an idea. Why don't you review the things we've done—the specials, the commercials, the whole magilla—and then when Andy gets here—he's due back, when, Monday?—you'll be up to speed and we can take a meeting not only about this but maybe also about not cutting back so much on new production. That was Jay's idea—you know, the bean counter?" He shook his head, tapped his temple. "People like that, I don't know where they're coming from."

He showed her how to use the tape player and its remote control, and how the tapes were more or less arranged—GC's own productions, news coverage of its activities, and documentaries on all kinds of related subjects. Movies too, some on records like LP's that used a different player.

"This is great!" she said, looking around. "You don't by any chance have *Gone With the Wind*, do you?"

"As a matter of fact we do," Craig said, smiling. "With screen tests and outtakes and a whole mess of other material."

"*Oh God!*" Rosemary cried. "*I'm in HEAVEN!*"

"**G**ood morning, may I ask who's calling?"—a pleasant female voice with just a hair of a Japanese L.

"This is Andy's Mom," she said. "He gave me this number."

"One moment please. Is this Rosemary E. Reilly speaking?"

"Yes," she said.

"Please hang up, Rosemary. Andy will return your call soon. If you wish him to call you at a different number, press one."

She hung up, suspecting she'd been talking with a computer chip. She'd have to watch *It's a Mad, Mad, Mad, Mad World*.

She punched the pillows up higher behind her, settled her glasses, took the other half of the croissant from the plate on the tray, what the hell, and nibbled while she checked the crossword puzzle. She did the upper-left-hand corner in her head and was refolding the paper one-handed to the book review when the phone rang. She dropped the paper and the croissant stub, licked crumbs from her fingertips, brushed them on satin, picked up. "Hello?"

"Hi, Mom, everything okay?"

"Couldn't be better!" she said. "Breakfast in bed! I feel like I'm in an MGM movie, the old MGM. Norma Shearer, *Garbo* . . ." She swooned on the satin.

He chuckled in her ear. "I think you'd make the cut."

Smiling, taking her glasses off, she said, "Where are you, angel?"

"In Rome, just the right place for one."

"You sound as if you're right around the corner."

"Wish I were. What's up?"

She said, "I don't mean to be pushy but I—"

"If it's about Craig and the commercial, I called him about something else and he mentioned it. I think it's a *great* idea."

She said, "You do?"

"Absolutely. Talk about someone coming to something with fresh eyes; who could possibly have fresher eyes than Rip Van Rosie? Not just about the commercials but about everything that's going on. You've put your finger on something I should have seen for myself weeks ago. We'll get right to work on it, you included. I'm sorry but I'm really in the middle of something. I'm coming back Saturday."

"*Saturday?*" she said.

"I canceled Madrid." A beat. "I never missed anyone before."

She watched a whole batch of GC commercials and specials—the medium's best, undoubtedly—handsomely produced, stirringly written and visualized, all featuring Andy. Sometimes when he was talking to her, about lightening up, lighting her candle, and so on, she could almost see a flicker of his old eyes in the new ones. She rewound, froze, and stepped the picture forward frame by frame a few times, but no, there was nothing—just his hazel eyes and her memory, seeing his beautiful tiger eyes in the wake of the kiss, the wicked, shocking kiss . . .

But really, could anyone blame him? Poor lonely angel . . .

And it wasn't as if she *looked* like his old mom. Every newspaper and magazine article and TV talking head—well it was vain even to *think* about what they had to say on that subject.

She watched, five or six times, a ten-second spot where he was his absolute Jesus best, strong and loving and just plain gorgeous, reminding her to pick up her candles at the supermarket or wherever and put them out of reach of the kids, and to wait and open the shrink-wrap along with everyone else in the world, just before the Lighting.

After that, as a break, she watched screen tests and outtakes from *Gone With the Wind.*

8

SHE WAS edgy Friday, thinking about Andy being thirty thousand feet in the air tomorrow afternoon.

And down on the ground tomorrow evening . . .

Around midafternoon she called Joe to arrange to go to the airport with him. "The spa, the fitness center, whatever," she said, "it's coed all the time, isn't it?"

"Unisex. Sure. When you thinking of going?"

"Now," she said. "I want to loosen up. I'm a little tense, with Andy flying tomorrow."

"Give me twenty minutes. I'll show you around and introduce the guys and make sure nobody pesters you."

She said, "I don't want anybody being shut out, Joe."

"It's just a question of cluing people in on how to behave, that's all. Don't worry."

"That's great," she said. "Thanks. Whenever you're ready. Don't rush."

They pedaled exercise bikes side by side. He told her about his ex-after-twenty-years, Veronica, in real estate now in Little

Neck, and his daughter, Mary Elizabeth, going for her master's in economics at Loyola. She told him about the proposed commercial and how pleased she was to be getting actively involved in GC. Both ideas sounded good to him.

She jumped rope, atrociously, while he punched a punching bag, awesomely. "I used to box," he said, dancing in and out, rat-a-tat-tatting. "Golden Gloves, middleweight."

"I used to jump rope," she said, untangling the damn thing from around her ankle. "Omaha Junior High School Championship Team, two years running."

"I can tell by your form," he said, rat-a-tat-tatting.

They strode along on side-by-side treadmills.

"Great place, isn't it?"

"Oh terrific," she said. "A real morale booster." A floodlit photo shoot was going on across the equipment-filled room. Small swimsuits on large young women.

Joe sneered and looked away, striding along. "Not my style," he said. "Ronnie was a fashion model when we started going together. The first time she turned sideways I called Missing Persons." He smiled at her. "My mother was a broomstick. You know how it is with us guys—'I want a girl, just like the girl, that married dear old Dad.'"

Striding along in place, Rosemary nodded. "Yeah, I know how it is," she said, "I know."

She was still edgy when she got back to the suite. She called Judy, who was home sounding teary. She jumped at the invite.

She arrived on the dot of eight, in a kerchief and a wool coat with damp shoulders, holding a big brown Bloomingdale's shopping bag. Under the coat the sari was peach; out of the bag came a plastic Scrabble board with a built-in turntable and molded nests for the tiles, a beaded drawstring bag, two black racks, a miniature silver-caged hourglass, and—naturally—a scorekeeping gizmo.

They set up on the table by the window. Light snow was falling, powdering the park's treetops, hazing Fifth Avenue's cliff of lights half a mile away. Rosemary won first move.

She looked through her glasses at JETTY IR on the rack— trying not to think of ice forming on wings and the damn timer at the side of the table (sand running out)—and lifted the tiles in clusters. She fed them into the nests across the board as JIT-TERY. "Double on the J," she said, "double word, fifty-point bonus."

Judy tapped at the gizmo—not with a special fingernail, just one of a set of matching pearl ovals. "One hundred," she said. "Good beginning."

"Thank you," Rosemary said, giving her an over-the-glasses look while drawing new tiles from the bag.

Judy turned the timer over, looked at the board through her mascara, blinked, and set tiles down below the J, making JINXED. "Double word," she said.

Rosemary plucked up tiles, reached without turning the board, and began laying in FOXY using the X and the pink space beside it.

Judy wailed and wept and tore at her hair. "*Now he's ruined my Scrabble too! Look what I did! An X by a pink! You win! You win! He's melted my brain! He's made my life SHIT! I'm jinxed! Jinxed by HIM! That's why I saw the word!*" She threw herself across the board sobbing, beating her fists on the table.

"Oh dear," Rosemary said, catching the rolling timer. She set it up straight and got up; moved to the side of the table and bent over Judy, patted her hair, stroked her heaving back. "Ah, Judy," she said, "ah, Judy . . . No guy is worth getting this upset about, not even oh jeez it's *Andy*, isn't it? Isn't it Andy? It is, isn't it?"

Yeses snuffled in among the sobs, yeses and Andys.

Rosemary nodded, sighed. She was getting slow. In her old age.

Judy raised herself from the board, weeping, tiles dropping from her cheek, the mascara holding up surprisingly well. "I *hate* Andy!" she cried, tearing her button away, tearing silk, flinging the button against the window. "I only wore it because I didn't want you to guess! I *hate* him! I'll make my own button to say how I really feel! Oh Rosemary, if you knew the whole story, if you knew what goes on up on the ninth—"

"Shh, shh." Rosemary hugged and soothed her. "Shh, calm down, dear," she said. "Ssh. Take a good, deep breath. That's it . . . Atta girl . . . There . . . That's a little better. Now why don't you go pat some cool water on your face and then we'll have a good long talk. Would you like something to drink? There's room service, so if you're hungry, just say so."

They sat on the sofa.

"He spoke at a benefit for Indian flood relief," Judy said, dabbing. "Last summer at Madison Square Garden. I brought a proposal I had written for improving methods of food distribution, and was able to hand it to him personally. Right then, there was a little spark between us."

Rosemary nodded, listening.

"A few days later," Judy said, "he called me here, to his office, and invited me to join GC, as a secretary at first but with the prospect, the promise, of going higher. We began a relationship—as equals—but within days, nights I should say, he gained complete mastery of me. You can't begin to imagine what an incredible lover he is."

"No," Rosemary said, "no, of course not, being his mother. No, I certainly can't. No."

"I meant that in the general sense," Judy said. She leaned closer to Rosemary. "In my culture," she said, "women readily confide in one another about intimate matters. I have two married sisters, and my roommates at Vassar liked nothing better than to discuss their sexual activities. So even though I've only known one other man myself—a slimeball named Nathan about whom the less said the better—I know that all men, not only he, are more concerned with their own satisfaction than that of their partners. And in truth, as the climax approaches, women are too, *n'est-ce pas*? Don't we all ultimately become involved solely with our own mounting excitement?"

Rosemary nodded.

"Not Andy," Judy said, and sighed. "It's as if a part of him is always in control, always aware of *me* and my needs and my feelings. *And now it's HER needs he's aware of, HER wretched feelings! I can't bear it!*" She grabbed at her hair.

Rosemary caught her wrists. "Whose?" she asked. "Who?"

"The woman he's in Rome with!" Judy cried. "And going to Madrid with! His new beloved! The woman he was with after your dinner on Thanksgiving, when I waited all night for his call! The one he took to the retreat for the weekend instead of me! There has to be someone! *Why else not a word, Rosemary, not a single WORD, in eight days and nights? Why else?*"

Rosemary stayed silent a moment. Shrugged. Said, "*I* don't know . . ."

"And if only that were the worst of it . . ." Judy drew a breath, shook her head, cast a sidelong look at Rosemary. "He led me into—practices I didn't even know were—"

"Stop right here," Rosemary said, pressing a hand on Judy's arm. "I really don't want to hear details. You're upset for no reason. He isn't going to Madrid; he's cutting the trip short because there's *someone here he misses very much*. He told me so yesterday morning."

"He did?" Judy stared at her.

Rosemary nodded. "Yes," she said. "He's coming back tomorrow. I'm absolutely certain he'll be calling you. I'll bet on it. And I'm sure he'll have a good reason for not having called you. I'll bet on that too."

"Oh, Rosemary, do you really mean it?" Judy asked. "Are you sure you're not saying this just so I'll feel better?"

Rosemary smiled at her. "Judy," she said, "I'm Andy's Mom. Would I lie to you?"

Judy shook her head, smiling. "No," she said, "no. Thank you, Rosemary! Thank you!" She dabbed at her eyes, sighed, shook her head. "Look at me," she said. "I was an intelligent, capable woman with a meaningful job to do—and he has me completely derailed, a blubbering ninny who puts an X by a pink."

Patting her hand, getting up from the sofa, Rosemary said, "Come on, we'll start over."

"No!" Judy said, getting up, going after her. "It wouldn't be fair, you had a hundred! It's easy to put back: you were 'jittery,' I was 'jinxed,' you were 'foxy.'"

Rosemary, sitting at the table, shook her head. "No, dear, a new game. I insist on it."

"Okay, but you go first."

As they gathered tiles, Judy asked, "Are you good at anagrams too?"

Rosemary recalled the time, weeks before giving birth, when she had shifted tiles back and forth between STEVEN MARCATO and ROMAN CASTEVET, realizing that the neighbor who had befriended them was the son of Adrian Marcato, the nineteenth-century Satanist who had lived at the Bramford. "Pretty good," she said.

"Thanksgiving night," Judy said, "while I was waiting for Andy's call, I finally solved the all-time killer anagram, after more than a year of working at it in trains and buses and waiting rooms." She sighed, smoothing her hair down. "Quite minuscule compensation, in truth."

"It *sounds* like a killer," Rosemary said, drawing tiles from the bag.

"That was an observation," Judy said. "The anagram is 'roast mules.'"

"'Roast mules'?"

"R, O, A, S, T," Judy said, turning the timer over, "M, U, L, E, S. They can be made into one common ten-letter English word, so common that even children of five and six use it."

Switching tiles around on the rack, Rosemary said, "I'll get on it later."

"Don't come begging for the answer," Judy said, drawing tiles from the bag. "You'll be wasting your breath; I'm unyielding. And no fair using a computer."

"I don't know how to," Rosemary said, "but I've really got to learn. What a great tool! Who ever thought they'd be so small and cheap? They filled whole rooms! Double on the Y, double word." Starting at the central pink space, she laid out the letters of DANDY.

9

HE BROUGHT her an angel—a curly-headed lad with a lyre and a book and a fine pair of wings, reclining in terra-cotta relief on a plaque about four inches square, white on della Robbia blue.

"Andrea della Robbia made it," he said. "Circa fourteen seventy."

"Oh my *God*, Andy!" she said, cradling it in both hands, adoring it. "It's the most beautiful thing I've ever seen!"

"It's named 'Andy,'" he said. "For him, I guess."

Smiling, she tiptoed to kiss his cheek. "Oh thank you, darling, thank you!" She kissed Andy della Robbia—lightly, *very* lightly. "My handsome angel Andy!" she said to it. "I adore you! I could eat you up!" She gave it another feather-kiss.

Sunday brunch was the first chance they had to be together. At the airport, he had come out of the VIP pass door with two elderly men. They seemed to be in an ongoing discussion, so after a hug and two handshakes outside the limo—one with a Chinese, one with a Frenchman—and a little eye language with Andy, she had ridden back to the city the way she had ridden out, up front with Joe. They listened to tapes of fifties big-band music, chatted about the musicians, and admired the billboards that had begun going up December first—Andy beaming at them over the lines of copy: *Here in New York we're lighting our candles at 7 p.m. on Friday, December 31st. Love ya!*

When they got out of the limo on the building's lower garage level—at two in the morning Rome time—Andy was jet-lagged. They made their morning date.

Rosemary and the waiter had shifted the Scrabble table aside a few feet to make room by the window for the brunch table and chairs. She walked there slowly, hands cupped, and leaned the plaque carefully, *very* carefully, against the side of the jam caddy—so Andy della Robbia could see and be seen.

Andy Castevet-Woodhouse, seated, smearing cream cheese on bagel, said, "You look great. That's just the kind of negligee I was picturing."

"I'm meeting Joe at the spa at eleven-thirty," Rosemary said in her pink sweatsuit and sneakers, sitting down.

He said, "Uh, you and Joe . . .?"

"Enjoy each other's company," she said, unfolding her napkin. "I would tell you to mind your own business, but I played Scrabble with Judy the other night so I'm not in a position to talk. Indian women sure do, at least the heartbroken, maltreated ones."

He groaned, filling her cup with steaming coffee.

"You really ought to be ashamed of yourself," she said, shaking a packet of sweetener at him. "She's such a nice girl. And what a champ! She beat me twice, and I'm good. I'm not used to a two-minute limit, not that that's an excuse. We're having a rematch tomorrow or Tuesday." She tore a corner from the packet.

"She no longer appeals to me," he said, lifting a slice of

salmon on the tines of a silvery fork. "What do you want me to do, fake something I don't feel?"

"You could at least have spoken to her face-to-face about it."

"Oh sure," he said. "You haven't seen her in her District Attorney mode." He laid the salmon over the cream cheese.

"I have a feeling you'd stand up under cross-examination," she said, stirring her coffee.

He bit and chewed, looking out the window.

She sipped, looking at the plaque. "It's just so *beautiful,* darling," she said. "Thank you *so much.*" She sighed, drew the basket of rolls and bagels nearer, poked among them.

Andy sighed. "You're right," he said. "It's not my finest hour. I'll call her later. She sleeps late Sundays anyway."

Rosemary chose a thin slice of bagel. "We're invited to a fund-raiser for cerebral palsy," she said. "*Against* it. You know. In the ballroom, Wednesday, black tie. I'm going with Joe. He says he's a great dancer; is he?"

Andy shrugged. "Pretty good," he said. Took a bite.

"I thought maybe you and Judy . . ."

"Mom," he said, chewing, "she doesn't *appeal* to me anymore. I can't help it. Okay? I wish I could."

She spread a thin layer of cheese onto her bagel slice, squinting at it. "Bring someone else," she said. "Does Vanessa have a steady?"

"I don't know," he said.

She took a small bite and chewed. "I did a little trading in the Bergdorf boutique," she said. "Six old-lady outfits for a satin sheath right off Ginger Rogers' back. I figure if Joe thinks he's Astaire, I'll humor him. I hope I didn't go overboard." She took a larger bite and chewed, peering out the window at something of interest.

Watching her, Andy smiled. "Aren't you the foxy one," he

said. "You win, we're a foursome. But after New Year's we're going on a little vacation alone, just the two of us. We're going to need it; we're going to be really busy all month." He wound the fork's tines around a sliver of salmon on his plate, frowning. "There's a real danger of the timing getting screwed up," he said. "We just got polls showing eleven percent of seniors worldwide still think the Lighting's at midnight everywhere. Can you believe it? We're going to have to do *something* more. And there's the PA commercial. I'd like to meet on it tomorrow at three; is that all right with you? Craig, Diane, and Hank. Maybe Sandy too; she comes up with good ideas."

"*You* know everybody, I don't."

He raised the forked curl of salmon and put it into his mouth, ate it facing her as she sipped.

She lowered the cup. "Don't do that," she said.

"Do what?"

"Just stick with the hazel, Mr. Wise Guy," she said. "I mean it, Andy. And don't tell me it was my imagination either."

Specific information on representative PA groups might be useful at the meeting, Rosemary realized, so she eased past Monday morning's Film Society meeting with a whispered "Hi, everybody"—to Craig, Kevin, Vanessa, Polly, and Lon Chaney Jr., sprouting face hair—and went right on into what she had begun to think of as her office. Craig's assistant Suzanne would be reclaiming it the Monday after New Year's but maybe they could share it, as long as there were two desks.

She searched among the news and documentary tapes, and was about to recruit a computer-literate research assistant when she found a tape of a year-old PBS production called *Anti-Andy*.

Watching it, she had some doubts about its overall objectivity—the narrator, a charming if loquacious Southerner, was wearing a large I ♥ ANDY button—but the footage he eventually got around to showing spoke concisely for itself, ranging from the foolish to the frightening.

The likeliest winner in the foolish division was the Ayn Rand Brigade, whose half-dozen sallow, crewcut members wore large dollar signs painted on their T-shirts and small ones tattooed below their sweat-bands. They opposed tax exemptions for religious institutions and supported "In Reason We Trust" on paper money—everybody's, not just the United States'. They had hijacked a freight train in Pittsburgh, tied banners to both sides of the engine reading PAY YOUR TAXES, ANDY AND ALL WITCH DOCTORS!, and driven it cross-country with their one female member at the throttle, a piece of symbolism based on one of Rand's novels but by and large meaningless to the general public. The train had been abandoned in Montana, where the Brigade was believed to have found refuge in an enclave of laissez-faire capitalists.

The middle ground of anti-Andy protesters was best represented by the ACLU, still around and still fighting the good fight. Their spokesman made it plain that he loved Andy and admired everything he had done to improve race relations, ease the abortion conflict, settle the Irish troubles, and get the Arabs and Israelis back yet again to the negotiating table. Good grief, wasn't he wearing *two* I ♥ ANDY buttons? He just felt that as long as Andy was addressing groups like the Joint Chiefs of Staff and the governors of all the states, then GC should be renamed WC, for World's Children, and if that was a problem in Europe, then EC for Earth's Children. And did Andy really have to lean quite so heavily on his resemblance to Jesus Christ?

Sheer rudeness. She was surprised at the ACLU.

The frightening anti-Andy group, the Smith Brothers, were frightening only to her. They had been joke fodder for late-night comedians; the Southerner showed samples.

Four mountain men more wildly bearded than their cough-drop namesakes, the Smith Brothers had holed up in a Tennessee cabin with the latest in military hardware, bullhorning to the world that Andy was the son of Satan, the Antichrist, and they weren't giving up without a fight.

The FBI had waited them out and they were now in a federal hospital, shaven, medicated, and undergoing psychiatric evaluation.

The meeting was hugely productive and over almost before it began. Seven took part—Andy, Judy (with memo gizmo), Diane, Craig, Sandy, Hank, and Rosemary—in Andy's office looking out at the buildings of Central Park South and midtown. The coffee table was stocked with veggies and nuts; they sat around it on a black leather sofa and chairs, Hank in his motorized wheelchair.

"*You were right, Rosemary!*" Judy had whispered on the way in, radiant in a buttercup sari, I ♥ ANDY-ed. "*A joyous reunion last night!*"

Rosemary was joyous for her.

And for Andy too, the lying weasel. *Mom, she doesn't appeal to me anymore, I can't help it, I wish I could.* She smiled at him, taking a carrot stick from the bowl he offered, smiling at her.

Everyone agreed about simple being better than elaborate, for both effectiveness and fast production, and from there it was a hop, skip, and jump to a unanimous decision to use the same technique that had produced four of Andy's top ten commercials—which meant that he and Diane would sit in a couple of easy chairs on the stage of the amphitheater down on the floor below, the ninth floor, and schmooze about the PA's and their rights for a couple of hours while Muhammed and Kevin worked the hand-held cameras. Diane would then be edited out and the footage pared down. And pared, and pared, and pared.

Except that this time, Diane suggested, Rosemary should do the schmoozing, her feelings on the subject obviously being stronger than Diane's. The PA's could all be shipped to the South Pole as far as she was concerned. Rosemary would also draw richer emotional responses from Andy. "And leave some of her in," Diane said. "She radiates honesty and openness."

Craig said, "What do you say, Rosemary, do you want to give it a shot? The most we can lose is a few hours tomorrow morning. Andy, I assume it's okay with you?"

From then on it was a party. Andy opened a bottle of wine, and William and Vanessa came in with another bottle. William, our ambassador to Finland under three presidents, was handsome and white-haired—red tie, white shirt, blue suit. A fun guy though, judging from his hand on Vanessa's miniskirted rump.

Yuriko and Polly came in—Rosemary had hardly spoken a word with either of them—and Muhammed and Kevin, fiddling with one of the cameras. Then Jay swooped in and the whole GCNY inner circle was there, all the varied team that was holding the fort or just hanging out during the generous year-end vacation—all thirteen of them.

Plus Rosemary. Sipping ginger ale, talking with Hank and Sandy about the Broadway season, such as it was, she saw Judy nearby eyeing her sadly but then radiant again, holding onto Andy's arm and smiling at him as he spoke with Jay—all aflutter about notes coming due in January. Rosemary had to smile too as Andy smoothed Jay's feathers, giving him his solemn word, right hand raised, that sufficient funds would be in place by the first business day of January to meet all of GC's legal obligations.

Diane called downstairs and ordered crab cakes and the little potato pancakes for fourteen.

Rosemary talked with Vanessa about motivational psychology, with Yuriko about computers, with Sandy and Polly about skin cream.

When the windows were alight on Central Park South, and the party was winding down, Diane sent Muhammed and Kevin and Polly down to make sure everything was spick-and-span on the ninth floor.

She talked with Craig a moment, then sent Yuriko and Vanessa down too.

Dapper in his tux, Joe Maffia talked with the band-leader a moment, then walked back around the rim of the jam-packed dance floor toward the center front table for twelve. The cha-cha ended sooner than was generally expected, and by the time Joe took Rosemary's hand and Andy stood up and took Judy's, the musicians had changed books and some of their instruments, and the bandleader was cuing them into an Irving Berlin medley.

When Andy and Judy and Rosemary and Joe walked onto the floor, everyone else backed off, clapping warmly but not excessively, forming an admiring circle within which the two couples orbited to "Let's Face the Music and Dance." Like in a movie.

Smiling at Joe, Rosemary said through her teeth, "Oh God look at them! They're *looking!* I can't *stand* this!"

"Just relax," Joe said, dipping her low, "I do all the work." He lifted her. "You got a real winner in this dress, Rosemary. It's perfect for ballroom. I only wish I'd worn my tails."

She relaxed, what choice? The glass of champagne she'd had helped, and Joe's arm and hand were surprisingly light.

"See what I mean?"

"Hey, Joe, you *are* great . . ."

"Ronnie and I went to Roseland twice a week," he said, easing up on the flash. "You want to go sometime? You could wear shades, plenty of people do."

"Let me work up to it."

"You're there."

Andy was a good dancer too, whirling white-saried Judy around with elegance and style—and what man *doesn't* look his absolute best in black tie? "I give him lessons now and then," Joe said, looking with her. "He had two left feet when we started."

"Last one in is a rotten egg!" Andy shouted over Judy's shoulder. The onlookers laughed—and hustled back onto the floor, jamming it again as the lights dimmed a point or two and the band segued into "Change Partners."

Rosemary breathed a sigh. "Sometimes I'm glad I had him," she said.

Joe, smiling, said, "He sure has a knack for saying the right thing at the right time, doesn't he? You think it's because he's the son of an actor?"

She drew a breath. "Who knows?"

"I didn't mean you didn't contribute too," he said. "You know, I'm surprised they haven't turned up anything on your ex since whatever year it was. It's like he—"

Andy tapped Joe's shoulder. "Change partners," he said. "Orders from Irving Berlin."

Rosemary and Judy smiled at each other as the four obeyed.

Andy favored a tighter hold and the lyrics in the ear:

"*Can't you see, I'm longing to be in his place? Won't you change partners, and dance with me?*"

"Crooning?"

"It comes under the heading of Great Communication. So does the dress." "Back *off*, are you *nuts*?"

He backed off, danced her angelically, devilishly grinning at her. Nodded at dancers alongside, said, "Love ya."

She caught her breath, gave him a look as he turned her.

He said, "Craig's going crazy trying to decide what to cut. Of you. He's already edited out all of me. Really, just about. We're going to call it the Andy's Mom commercial."

"Love you both!" a girl of eight or nine called to them, dancing by on Dad's shoes. "We're lighting our candles at Colonial Williamsburg!"

"Love *you*, darling!" Rosemary called after her.

"Love ya, sweetheart!" Andy called. He smiled at Rosemary. "You want to do another one?" He dipped her low. "About when to light the candle in which time zone?" Lifted her.

"I'd love to," she said. "In fact, I'm thinking about starting a whole career."

"Don't," he said. Smiled at her.

"Why not?" she asked him. "I'm the Great Radiator, aren't I? Wasn't I radiating yesterday? My New Year's resolution is to start radiating independent income, with some kind of interview program. Every network has invited me to lunch; I'm going to start accepting."

Looking at her, turning with her, he said, "You don't want to give too much weight to those guys. One day they're hot, the next day they're cold."

She drew back and squinted at him.

His shoulder shrugged under her hand. He said, "I just

don't want you getting your hopes up too high, that's all." He looked away.

"Oh come *on,*" she said. "Get real, Andrew. They'll be panting the minute I say I'm interested and they won't cool down either. You know that's the truth."

He looked back at her. Nodded. "I guess," he said.

" 'Guess'?"

"We're naming our twins Andrew and Rosemary!" a woman sang out alongside them, her green-gowned belly immense; her man chimed in with, "Love you both!" The band launched into "Blue Skies."

"Oh bless you," Rosemary said, swaying with Andy. "Bless *them!* Love you!" She tugged the hair at Andy's nape; he looked at the couple. Said "Love ya"—and watched them as they were borne away among other dancers.

Rosemary sighed, smoothed his hair down, rested her cheek on his shoulder. Sang softly as they turned together, "*Nothing but blue skies, from now on. Never saw the sun shining so bright . . .*"

Andy looked out over her head. Shook his own head as if to clear it. Smiled at the people dancing around them.

Outside the door of Rosemary's suite, Joe's palms hovered *this close* to her bare shoulders. "Andy's Mom," he said. "I can hardly believe it."

The concierge was absent from his desk down the hall. Perhaps he had been clued in that it was a good time to go take a leak.

"Joe," Rosemary said, "sometimes I lose sight of it myself, but Andy's not Jesus and I'm not Mary. I'm Rosemary Reilly, from Omaha. The men in the family work for Hormel. Or used to."

He took a breath. "Gotcha," he said, and grabbed her shoulders and kissed her mouth. She kissed him back, holding him.

They smiled at each other, and she got the card from her bag and unlocked the door. They went in.

She let him go ahead of her, bolted the door behind her.

Why bandy? She was randy. He was handy.

They got snifters and two miniatures of Rémy Martin from the bar and sat on the sofa with the lights down low. Hugged and kissed each other.

A lot.

"I have to tell you something," Joe said, caressing her cheek. "I haven't exactly been celibate since Ronnie and I split, so considering all the crap around, I think I'd better get myself checked out before we get into—you know, anything risky. But I've got a suggestion I'd like to make."

"What's that?" she asked.

"Well, I'm thinking about New Year's Eve," he said. "I know we're all going to light our candles together, either at the ceremony in the park or at Gracie Mansion or someplace, but I thought that maybe later, at midnight, you and I could light candles, just the two of us. I've got extras."

She smiled at him, and said, "That's a great idea, Joe." They kissed each other.

He took the snifters from the coffee table and gave her hers. "I figure we can start the year off with a bang," he said, smiling. "That's a pun that's intended." He sipped his brandy, watching her.

She smiled, sipped hers. Said, "If not at the beginning of the year 2000, when?"

He smiled at her. Nodded. "When you stop to think about it," he said, "I'll bet you a higher percentage of people are going to be screwing around right after the Lighting than at any other time in all human history."

"You're right," she said. "The year 1000, forget it." They chuckled.

"Dullsville!" he said. They pecked each other's lips. "Jeez," he said, shaking his head, "this is something I really didn't anticipate!"

"I did," she said. "The first good look I got at you, I thought, 'old but sexy.'"

"Thanks a heap, Rosemary."

"I was thirty-one in my head," she said. "I still am sometimes."

He said, "You're about eighteen in your mouth."

They got rid of the snifters.

10

SHE WOKE up bright and early, feeling fully recharged despite the smooching till midnight.

Or because of it, more likely. She'd damn near forgotten how exciting two-party sex could be, even with Joe's sensible and admirable limitations. Her first real contact with a man in . . . almost seven years *her* time, add twenty-seven for reality. Ye gods.

The Kiss didn't count, of course.

She looked forward to New Year's Eve with Joe.

Today was what—Thursday, the ninth? She'd have to speak to him. How long did it take to get checked out? And exactly how romantic did they have to be, time-wise?

Her New Year's resolution would have to wait for its proper season; more important things came first, like helping make sure everyone got the Lighting right, time-wise.

Again, as whenever she gave more than passing thought to the event, the happening, its beauty and symbolic power thrilled her. She had only learned on Tuesday, during the schmoozing and taping, about the high-resolution satellite images that would be coming back to Earth as the candles were lighted, about the concert—the Boston Pops, the Mormon Tabernacle Choir— that would be broadcast live in worldwide stereo. Maybe Andy was no angel but he was certainly an artist, because that's what his Lighting was: a major work of conceptual art, accessible and meaningful to all humanity.

He was nuts, of course—weren't so many of them?—rubbing against her like that right out there among the dancers; a dozen people must have—*Anywhere!* He shouldn't have done it *anywhere!* She really had to have another talk with him.

Opening the draperies, she got a golden sun smack in the eye; raised an arm against its brilliance above the Fifth Avenue cliff. *Never saw the sun shining so bright!*

Never saw so many joggers either. She squinted down under her forearm at two lanes of shorts and sweatsuits, jogging in both directions beyond the southbound taxis and cars on the Park Drive. Who'd have imagined there were so many health nuts crazy enough to be out running early on a cold December morning, under a blue sky, then going on to put in a full day's work . . .

Never saw things going so right! In leotards and a sweatsuit, Garboed up in a muffler, a floppy-brimmed hat, and a big pair of shades—sunglasses till that very morning—she jogged with the health nuts, an incredibly attractive assortment of determined-looking New Yorkers, most of them sporting I ♥ ANDY buttons, a few in I ♥ ANDY sweatshirts, others declaring their ♥ for MOZART, CHOCOLATE, and FIRE ISLAND.

Noticing the days hurrying by! When you're in love—she segued into humming.

And saw, to her surprise—across the drive and beyond the park, on Central Park West—the Bram. Its peaked roof and upper turrets anyway, screened by tree branches. Or *was it* the Bram? The little she could see looked different somehow. Lighter.

She waited till the taxis and cars were checked by a traffic light farther north, and crossed the drive.

She followed a road that sloped up, curving rightward; walked its verge, cars passing close on her left. Nearing Central Park West, the road curved leftward and the whole of the Gothic brick building came into view. The Bramford, all right.

It had been cleaned up—sandblasted, or steamed, or whatever they were doing nowadays. Black Bramford had become Pale Peach Bramford. The gargoyles were gone; the stars and stripes waved atop the roof's pinnacle.

Andy's Boyhood Home.

Smiling, she shook her head. T-shirts were probably on sale in the courtyard—an assortment of Andy and one each of Theodore Dreiser and Isadora Duncan. Did they have any shirts with pictures of Adrian Marcato and his mementos of Satan? Of the Trench sisters sautéing sweet Daphne? Of Pearl Ames and her pets?

A woman sobbed behind her.

She turned, and saw, beyond a slatted snow fence and a span of shrubbery, a clearing lower down where a few people stood in a circle. The sobbing woman, young, in black, was being led away from the gathering by an older woman.

Rosemary shut her eyes. Sliding her fingertips in under her glasses, she pressed tight at her eyeballs, swaying.

The Unthinkable, the one thought she had stopped herself from even *thinking* of thinking about from the very first moment she'd seen Andy on TV *exactly a month ago today*—the Unthinkable tapped her on the shoulder.

She lifted her head, lowered her shades, brushed the Unthinkable's hand away. Tugged her hat down snug, wound her muffler over her mouth, and went looking for a path to the clearing.

She found one bending back from the road she'd been on, an asphalt lane curving down past a sign, *Strawberry Fields*, to where six or seven people stood around a wide black-and-white-patterned disc set in the ground, a few flowers and folds of paper on it. Some of the men and women looked down, as if praying; others gazed mournfully ahead. Other people, farther away, aimed cameras at the gathering, came closer aiming their cameras at the disc, clicking at it.

A stately Mediterranean-looking woman spilled an armful of red roses onto the disc, her eyes closed, her red lips moving. She was all in black like the younger woman, who sat, still sobbing, with her mother or whoever, on one of the surrounding benches.

Rosemary tried to stay calm, sure she was having some kind of vision, as the Unthinkable chiseled itself into her head: ANDY IS 33—THE SAME AGE AS JESUS WHEN HE WAS NAILED TO THE CROSS. *These people across from Andy's boyhood home were gathered around a shrine that didn't exist yet. But would someday.*

She drew a deep breath and walked closer to it, hands clenching at her sides.

The disc was a mosaic of black and white tiles, its pattern a wheel with curiously jagged spokes. At its center a four-letter word lay inset in black capitals amid the mass of red roses; she raised the glasses to be sure of it—MAGI.

What it signified she couldn't imagine, what wise men were being invoked or heralded and why. But did it matter? She lowered the glasses and walked on past the mourners, fixing her hat and muffler; walked faster down another path leading toward the drive, jogged down it seeing the top of the gold-glass tower half a mile away, bumping into someone, jogging on. She called back over her shoulder, "*I'm sorry, excuse me!*"

An oldster in a Yankees cap and an I ♥ SYMBOLS sweatshirt shook a fist after her. "*Watch where you're going, Greta Garbo!*"

She slowed herself down at the drive, waited, and jogged across into the southbound lane.

Jogged in the stream of joggers toward Andy in the tower of blinding gold sunshine.

He had told her Tuesday that her card had been validated for the lobby entry to the private elevator; she hadn't expected to make use of it. She touched 10, rocketed upward. It was still early, but he was usually at his desk by eight, he and the media said.

He was there this morning. When she was halfway through his quarter floor of empty cubicles with barren desks, she heard him speaking to someone doggedly, trying to get a word in. As she neared the open door to his anteroom, she heard him clearly. "Please? Please? Will you—*Hey! Please!* Just let me finish, okay? Half the billboards aren't even up yet, *more* than half in China and South America, but they're *all going to be up by Friday the latest*, everywhere."

She went into the anteroom—Judy wasn't at her desk yet—and went on across the anteroom toward the open door of Andy's office. "We're absolutely saturating TV from Monday the thirteenth right through to the end of the month with the two commercials you yourself said got the point across most clearly, the kid and his grandfather and—You *did!* Just the other day! Oh *shit . . .*"

She could see his hand raking through his tawny hair above the chair back as he sat facing the window behind his desk. She put hat and glasses into one hand, raised the other to the door—and paused, not wanting to interrupt him. Sniffed coffee.

"The numbers are going to get better, I promise you, I honestly don't think it's necessary or practical, and it just doesn't seem like the right thing to—Well of *course* she'll want to, I know that." His chair turned around and he looked at her.

She stepped into the office, turning her hands out apologetically.

He smiled, beckoned. "René," he said to the phone, standing up in a GC sweatshirt and jeans. "Excuse me. Excuse me. *René*, my mother just came in, could we cut it short, please?" He came around to the side of the desk as she came farther into the office. "Yes," he said. "I will." He said to her, "He says *bonjour*. The airport."

"Oh," she said, recalling the elderly Frenchman whose hand she had shaken. She waggled fingers.

"Mom says *bonjour* back," he said, eye-smiling at her. "We'll talk when you're home, okay? Have a good flight. And please, thank Simone for the generous offer and tell her I wish there were time to schedule a *dozen* more concerts. *Ciao* to the lovely granddaughters." He put the phone down. "Whew," he said, coming to her, wiping his hands back over his brow and hair. "Thanks for rescuing me. He's one of our main supporters and a sweet old guy but what a worrier!" He wiped his hands on his jeans. "And his wife is the world's worst soprano."

He held her shoulders, kissed her cheek.

She leaned against him, her cheek against his shoulder, held him, listened to his heart beating as his arms enclosed her. He said, "You're cold; were you running outside?"

"Mm-hmm," she said, staying close against him.

"With Joe?"

"Alone."

"And nobody bothered you?"

She raised the hand with the hat and glasses.

He drew back, looked down at her. "What's wrong?" he asked.

She said, "I've been worrying about you." Looked up at him. "I'm afraid—something awful might happen to you . . ."

He sighed, nodded. "It's possible," he said. "Awful things happen to awful people all the time. Look at Stan Shand. Kersplat."

"Oh *don't,*" she said, hitting his arm.

He said, "Did you have something particular in mind?"

"No," she said. "I just got scared. Up across from the Bram . . ." She looked at him.

"Did you see what they did to it?" he asked.

She nodded.

"I feel guilty about it," he said. "*That* isn't what scared you; what did? I can see you're upset . . ." He stroked her back.

She said, "I saw . . ."

"What?" he asked, stroking, looking down at her.

She shrugged, sighed. "Just a man with an anti-Andy sign . . ."

"An 'Original Son of Liberty'?" he said. "They're a joke, like the Ayn Rand Brigade. Don't worry, I'm as safe or unsafe as the next guy. Safer. Everybody loves me, remember?"

"If people found out . . ." She looked at him.

"Don't tell," he said, "I won't. Want some coffee? I just got a pot. Nice and fresh."

She sighed and said, "I'd love some."

He kissed her head and they let go of each other. She unwound her muffler as he went to the side table by the desk. "Go with Joe next time," he said. "Or me; I keep meaning to jog. Or with security. If someone recognized you, you could have been mobbed."

"Okay," she said, sitting on the sofa. She rubbed her hands.

He brought her a GC mug of coffee lightened to the right shade, with a spoon and a packet of sweetener. "Actually, I was going to call you in a few minutes," he said, sitting down in a side chair with a mug of his own. "Before René," he said, nodding toward the desk, "I was talking with Diane. She's had one of her theatrical brain-storms, but it's nothing essential and you shouldn't feel any pressure to do it, I really mean that. If you want to get right onto your own plans next week, I can have Judy set up appointments for you with the networks or you could—"

"Cut to the chase, Andy," she said.

"We go to Ireland," he said. "Next week for a few days. Dublin and Belfast. Because of your Irish roots and my lightening up the IRA. The idea is, they'll go more ape over us there than anywhere else and it'll get maximum coverage worldwide, maybe GCUK can get the King to move up his visit, and we'll mention the time-zone thing every five minutes. I can see this is going to be a hard sell."

She sat back, blinked a few times, and squinted at him, putting her mug down. "Of *course* I want to do it," she said. "Andy, I don't understand you." She leaned close to him, took his hands. "You act as if we're selling *cigarettes*," she said. "We're promoting a wonderful, beautiful event that's going to stir and excite the entire world! Don't minimize it; the Lighting is a work of *art*. I mean that. We had *lots* of artist friends, Guy and I, and some of them created 'happenings,' public events that people participated in and were enriched by, so I know what I'm talking about. The Lighting is going to be the greatest happening ever."

Andy sighed. "Okay, Mom," he said, "I'll stop minimizing it."

"Of *course* we'll go to Ireland," she said. "I always meant to someday." She shook her head. "How I wish Brian and Dodie weren't on that cruise . . ."

"It'll just be the two of us," he said.

She looked at him.

He smiled at her. "That was the champagne last night," he said. "Otherwise I never would have rubbed against you like that. I'll behave. Really." He tiger-flashed.

"My angel Andy," she said, and thought a moment while he waited, watching her. "No," she said, "I'm definitely going to need a secretary at my side. Preferably someone I know and have a rapport with. Any suggestions?"

He sighed and said, "Not off the top of my head, but I'll try to think of someone."

"Good," she said. "And my boyfriend comes too."

He looked at her. Said, "Your boyfriend?"

She nodded. "That's the way we big stars travel." She smiled, batting her lashes at him.

He didn't seem amused.

11

ON MONDAY morning, December 20th, the day after they got back from Ireland, Judy hitched up the skirt of her sari, said "Excuse me, gotta run," and cut in front of Hank's wheelchair to chase after Rosemary down the tenth-floor center hallway.

She caught up with her outside the ladies' room and pulled her in. "Rosemary, I've got to talk to you," she said, closing the door. She crouched, checked under stall doors, and stood up, catching her breath, smoothing her sari.

"My gosh, Judy," Rosemary said, rubbing her arm. "From *I Walked with a Zombie* to this? I'm glad you've recovered."

"I'm sorry," Judy said. "About the way I behaved—it was all I could do to get through the trip—and for hurting you now. I'm so anxious to get out of here. I'm leaving. Please, can we get together this evening? We must!"

"*Leaving?*" Rosemary said.

Judy nodded. "Leaving GC, leaving New York."

"Oh *Judy*, I know you and Andy have problems—"

"Had," Judy said. "It's over. I knew it the second night in Dublin. Remember? That was the night he had the fever, after you and he got caught in the rain—where was it, in the park?"

Rosemary nodded.

Judy sighed. "He used to like it when I had to play nurse or Mommy—all men do, or so I hear—but that night he—oh, I'll tell you later. Please, you *have* to make time. There's too much to tell you now, and I *have* to tell you before I go. And I want your counsel too about certain things."

"Judy," Rosemary said, "in *my* culture, which is basically Omaha with a thin overlay of New York, women really don't like hearing details about their sons' private affairs."

"It's nothing like that," Judy said. "Not in the sense you mean. It involves matters you'll be reading about anyway, in April or May, if not sooner."

Rosemary looked at her. "What do you mean?" she asked.

"I'll tell you everything later," Judy said. "And I beg you, don't tell Andy I'm leaving. I'll call him tomorrow or late to-night, but I'll never make the break if I have to face him. He gives me his soul-searching looks and romantic words and completely derails me every time; I despise myself for it."

Rosemary drew a breath, and said, "Okay. Tonight. Eight o'clock?"

"Thank you," Judy said, taking her hands, clasping them. "Thank you."

They went out into the hallway. Hank sat waiting a few yards away, his moon face aglow, his eyes twinkling behind his glasses. "Okay, Rosemary," he said, "let's have the scoop about you and the King!"

Judy said, "Oh yes please! I intended to broach the subject!"

"There is *no scoop whatsoever,*" Rosemary said. "You know those Brit reporters, so-called. He kissed my hand; what was he supposed to do, slap me?"

"Oh well," Hank said, "there's fun news here. I've got the weekend poll results."

"They're good?" Rosemary asked.

Judy, touching her shoulder, said, "They're great. See you later." She kissed Rosemary's cheek, said "Hank . . ."

"Take care," Rosemary said, and moved closer to Hank's chair.

"For the first full week the commercial's been running," Hank said, " 'Make them light candles' is down from an average of twenty-two percent to thirteen. Look."

"I don't believe it," Rosemary said, bending to read printouts. She whistled, read.

Hank smiled, watching her. He leaned his head side-ways, said, "Hi."

Rosemary turned, standing straight, and said "Hi" to Sandy in the ladies' room doorway—serene and blond in high-collared beige, even more Tippi-Hedren-in-*The-Birds* than usual. She must have been in one of the farthest stalls—too far away, surely, to have overheard what Judy had said.

Coming out smiling, Sandy said, "*Hello.* Welcome back. I was hoping you wouldn't be too jet-lagged to come in. What an exciting trip that must have been! You were a vision in the Belfast gown."

"See you later," Hank said, wheeling around and heading up the hallway.

"All right, *give!*" Sandy said, coaxing Rosemary with both red-nailed hands. "What's with His Majesty?"

"*Absolutely nothing,*" Rosemary said. "You know those Brit reporters, so-called."

They followed after Hank's chair, their heads close together.

Craig came down the hallway. He and Hank played at blocking and pushing, then Hank showed him the printouts and everybody huddled over them a minute or two.

Then Rosemary waved and went into the TV division, Hank rode on up the hallway, and Craig headed for the men's room. Sandy stayed where she was. "Craig," she said. "We have to talk when you're through."

One of the strangest things to the fresh eyes and ears of Rip Van Rosie was the way everybody in 1999 wrote and talked about terrorists *claiming responsibility* for their atrocities. Sister Agnes would have split her ruler and deepened the scars in her desk: "We *claim* that which is good!" *Whap!* "*Responsibility* implies intelligence and maturity!" *Whap!* "They're *admitting guilt!*" *Whap!* "*Shame* on those who say otherwise!" *Whap!*

Though Andy had cooled terrorism way down from last year's terrible peak, acts of violent barbarity still occurred, and not only in the Middle East. The morning they landed in Belfast, they had learned that over six hundred people in Hamburg had been killed by a new variant of an old terrorist gas. No one had yet "claimed responsibility." The affected area, a dozen square blocks near the harbor, was still toxic. Details were being withheld.

Rosemary had spoken to Andy on the plane home about the possibility of his doing a commercial or speech aimed at getting everyone to stop speaking Terrorist, so that those of them remaining and growing up would be goosed in the direction of thinking Civilized. He had agreed it was a good idea for next year, but he hadn't sounded wildly enthusiastic, so she was putting together some thoughts on possible approaches she'd stored in her memo gizmo, with the aim of either getting him more stirred up or doing something herself on the subject somewhere down the line.

That was what she really wasn't concentrating on while she waited for him to call about the nine-point drop in "Make them light candles." That's radiation!

He was busy with someone. He had to have seen the print-outs by now.

After another half hour or so, she called him—and got his recorded message.

She called Hank and got *his* message.

She got up to speak to Craig. Opened the door and goggled.

No Film Society!

No Craig, no Kevin, no nobody . . .

Nothing on the three TV's; how's *that* for weird?

She moved out amid the empty cubicles, where, if she cocked an ear and squinted, she could usually detect signs of life in the central hallway and the legal division beyond—a shift of light, a footfall, the far-off artillery of a computer game . . .

Not today.

Stillness unbroken.

She went back into the office.

Called Sandy, got *her* message.

She looked at the date of the *Times*—Monday, December 20, 1999 (HAMBURG DEATH TOLL MOUNTS . . .)—and finally realized why everybody had taken off so mysteriously.

And why she should take off too. Right now.

Only five more shopping days till Christmas.

In her shades and a kerchief, dark sweater, and slacks, she
browsed the Christmas-decorated windows of the lobby boutiques. Bellmen waved white-gloved fingers; she waved back,
paused for a laugh and a word. "You know those British reporters . . ."

She had sent sweaters from Dublin to her whole list of sib-
lings, siblings-in-law, nephews, and nieces—but that still left
everyone here to find gifts for: the GC crew (seven men, five
women), a few members of the hotel staff who had earned
more than just cash in an envelope (two men, two women),
and Andy and Joe.

Andy, of course, had presented a problem.

Last Christmas had been a breeze—a tricycle, jigsaw puzzles, and a couple of Dr. Seuss books. This Christmas, a little
over six months later, was different somehow, with him nearly
twenty-eight years older and knowing who his real father was.
Not a problem of what, but of whether.

Give *him* a present for *His* birthday?

Yes, she had decided. In a way it was like the don't-speak-Ter-
rorist thing: keep him aware of the alternative.

She priced gloves in the Gucci boutique, costume jewelry
at Lord & Taylor, cologne at Chanel.

In the Hermès boutique she picked out half a dozen ker-
chiefs and a scarf. She would give the scarf to Judy tonight—if
she couldn't get her to change her mind about leaving. Couldn't
she and Andy stay friends? (And what had she meant by
that unsettling "matters you'll be reading about anyway, in
April or May"?)

She paid with her credit card, reminding herself that regardless of who had planned and initiated GC—and let's
not think about *him* at this time of year!—its funding today
came mainly from plutocrats like René What's-his-*nom*, who

also contributed to a separate fund earmarked specifically for Andy's personal expenses; he had told her about it when he had given her the card, before they left for Ireland. No one in his or her right mind expected people today to identify with and be guided by someone who didn't live well. Get real, Mom. As for the dimes and dollars, and pesos et cetera that came in to GC's offices, that money all went entirely to local social programs and expenses; the IRS and its foreign cousins saw to that.

Okay. But she looked forward to Christmas shopping with her own money next year.

In the Sulka boutique she examined a handsome black satin robe trimmed and lined in royal blue that would be super on Andy. Wildly expensive, of course, and maybe a little too bedroomy, but a possibility . . .

She got back to the suite a little after four, having kept a two-thirty appointment for a hair touch-up and questions about the King. She'd barely gotten the shades off when the private line beeped; Andy had been trying to reach her.

"Hi, I wasn't going to bother you with this but then I remembered, wasn't *Luther* one of the plays Andy's father was in on Broadway?" Diane, an assumer-you-know-the-voice.

Rosemary said, "Yes . . ."

"I thought so. You may want to give these kids a hand. They're doing a revival of it, off-Off-Broadway, just started rehearsals. It turns out the owner of the space is a Lutheran; he says it's heresy and he's kicking them out on some technicality. The check was two seconds late."

"If he's a Lutheran why does he think it's heresy?" Rosemary asked. "It's a pro-Luther play."

"Do I know what's in the man's head? All I know is they've got two days before they're out on the sidewalk, they're having some kind of rally, and the director is the granddaughter of an old friend. If you could give them five minutes on freedom of speech, it would get them on the news and in the papers and save the day. That's the theory. Frankly I don't think the landlord will budge; he's pulled crap like this before and gotten away with it."

Rosemary said, "*Where and when is this rally?*"

She called Judy at her apartment. Got her message and held on. After the beep she said, "Judy, this is Rosemary. Could we possibly—"

"I'm here, Rosemary. What is it?"

"Hi," she said. "Could we possibly make it a little later tonight? There's this rally for some kids who are putting on a show . . ." She explained.

"Yes, of course! Help them! What a terrible thing when people try to stop the expression of ideas! Although, if the check was late and the man owns the property—"

"I'll be back by nine, according to Diane," Rosemary said, "but it's on Carmine Street in the Village so let's say nine-thirty to be safe."

"That's fine for me. I'm packing; I can use the time."

"Don't be in such a hurry," she said. "Let's talk a little."

"My mind is made up. Speak well. What do they say? Break a leg."

She called Diane. Said only a low-pitched "Okay."

"Oh good. It just may work; wouldn't *that* be nice. I'll arrange for a car. Seven-thirty?"

"I'm going to call Joe," she said. "If he wants to go, he may want to give his own car a workout. I'll call back. Have you seen Andy today?"

"I haven't seen anyone except my maid. I'm in bed with sciatica."

"Oh, I'm *sorry*, Diane!"

She called Joe at his apartment.

"Yeah, sure. We can use my car. Will *he* be there?"

"Andy?"

"The Lutheran."

"Joe," she said.

"Maybe we have some friends in common, that's all. I know theater owners. What time?"

She called Diane and got the address. "Your contact is the stage manager, Phil something. Oh, and congratulations on the polls!" The buzzer buzzed, Andy's buzz.

"Andy's here now," Rosemary said. "I'll let you know how it goes."

"Give him my—"

She clapped the phone down and hurried to the door as Andy buzzed again. She opened and roses came at her, rose-smelling roses round and red like the roses surrounding MAGI.

Andy beamed at her—too brightly? "Count them," he said, giving her the bundle of stems wrapped in the lobby florist's gold paper.

"They're beautiful," she said, cradling the bouquet, "thank you"—watching his face as he came in and closed the door. "Is something wrong?" she asked.

"You jest," he said. "Count them."

Nine.

"For the nine-point drop," he said. "That's radiation!"

"That's what *I* thought!" They pressed cheeks, kissed them. "Oh thank you, darling," she said, "they really are beautiful!" She nuzzled her face in the roses.

"Your hair looks different," he said, unzipping his jacket.

"You like it? Ernie got inspired." She showed him both sides.

Squinting, his head cocked, he said, 'Mmmmm . . . it's
going to take a *teeny* bit of getting used to."

"I love it," she said, opening the kitchen as he took his
jacket off and dropped it. "Where've you been all day?" She
opened a cabinet.

"The Mayor flew a bunch of us up to Albany," he said, "to
beg the Governor about the hospital bill."

She got out a cut-glass vase. "And that's how you dressed?"

"Yeah," he said. Nodded. "And boy, was the Governor pissed
off." They smiled at each other. He leaned against the counter,
watching her as she put the roses into the vase. He said, "The
thing I had on for tonight was canceled. You want to go to a
movie?"

"Can't," she said, leaning back, squinting. "I'm speechify-
ing, briefly." She explained, jockeying the roses.

He said, "I'd love to hear you."

"Come on along," she said, "but Joe's taking me in his car.
"It's a two-seater, isn't it?"

"Three," he said.

Running water into the vase with the spray hose, she looked
at him and said, "On one condition."

"What's that?"

"Not one 'old buddy,' 'old man,' or 'old pal,'" she said. "Not
one in the entire evening."

"What are you *talking* about?" he said. "I don't—"

"Oh *Andy,*" she said, wiping the vase, "*honestly!* I really
expect a little more subtlety from you. You know perfectly well
what I mean."

"All right," he said, walking away toward the TV, "all right,
all right . . ."

"I'm going inside," she said, carrying the vase to the coffee
table. "I want to rest and make some notes. If you're staying,

there's half a ham-and-Swiss in the fridge. Or just take it with you if you want. I'm going to order something around six. Joe's coming at seven-thirty."

"Here's Van Buren." Andy stood at the TV, holding the remote. "Did you hear? He cut both gun lines out of his stump speech."

"Because of the *commercial?*" she asked.

"He reads polls."

Mike Van Buren, in a cowboy hat, against a blue sky, his breath pluming, said above several hand-held microphones, "—sides can cool down a little, don't you? The Original Sons of Liberty now say that if they're not being pushed, they'll reconsider lighting, so it really does look as if, thanks to Rosemary's thoughtful, heartfelt message, and Andy's too of course, we're all coming together as a nation."

Andy clapped his chest. "My career is over!" he cried.

Laughing, Rosemary said, "Oh God, he's moving toward the center; he'll be the next president because of us!"

Chuckling, channel-hopping, Andy said, "No way, I promise you."

"You never know in politics," she said.

"Trust me on this one," he said.

12

A TRULY hellish night.

The speech was just about the only thing that went well. The audience was smaller than Rosemary had expected—about thirty young men and women, the actors in the show and their friends—but they couldn't have been more responsive and supportive; it was almost as if they were her partners in some kind of reading or rehearsal or happening. The space was a four-story brownstone's ground floor, its platform stage smaller than the half-moon in GC's amphitheater. Squeezing even a minimal *Luther* onto it was going to be a real challenge for Diane's friend's granddaughter (who was having a detached retina repaired at St. Vincent's, Phil the stage manager said).

Rosemary got easy laughs quoting some of Hutch's put-downs of religious-fundamentalist library purifiers—he'd had a run-in with them over a scene in one of his boys' adventure books where the boys went skinny-dipping and sat around the campfire eating beef jerky—and thanks to an assist from the information line of the New York Public Library, she was able to quote accurately from Tom Paine and Tom Jefferson too. She preached effectively to the converted, who gave her a really big hand then gathered round for autographs, congratulating her and telling her she was great and to go for it and things like that. Andy sat in a back corner of the room on one of the plastic stack chairs, his legs out and crossed at the ankles, his arms folded, his head lowered. Joe, next to him, beamed at Rosemary, giving her two thumbs up and Andy an elbow.

The hellishness came before and after.

First there was the fire a few blocks east of Carmine Street—big enough to attract all approaching TV mobile units.

Then, at eight-thirty, when Phil said they would wait no longer and make do with the footage from the video-cams in the audience, just as everyone was getting seated again and he was raising his hands for silence—came the police cars.

And the bomb squad. With the truck and the dogs.

A warning had been phoned in by someone representing a group called Lutherans Against Luther—the play, not the man, the woman had specified. They were claiming responsibility for a bomb that was going to go off at nine o'clock. Ninety-nine chances out of a hundred it was a hoax but the entire building had to be evacuated immediately and searched from top to bottom. Sorry, folks.

Joe was ready to go get the car but Rosemary was more irked than ever at the incredible selfishness of some people who claimed to believe in Jesus Christ; and besides, being psyched up and having a sympathetic audience on tap, she felt the speech could be a good warm-up or tryout for longer speeches to tougher audiences.

Andy shrugged.

Joe said, "You're the boss"—to her, not him.

She borrowed Phil's phone—he was young and cheerful,

with wide-set blue eyes like Leah Fountain's, the same weak chin too—and backed across the crowded blocked-off street to the lee of a deli window, wrapping her coat more tightly around her. Everybody else—Andy, Joe, Phil, the actors, half of Carmine Street—was checking out the men and women coming down from the building's top two floors, Dominique's Dungeon.

Flexible standards, that rat-fink landlord. She shook her head, waiting through Judy's message. "It's Rosemary," she said. "Are you there?" She ought to have been; her apartment on West End Avenue was only a short walk from the Tower. "There's no way I'm going to be back by nine-thirty," Rosemary said, craning to see who or what the crowd was cheering. "We've had a bomb scare. Ten o'clock is more likely. I'll call the desk and tell them to tell whoever's on seven to let you in, in case I'm not back by then."

She did that.

It was well past nine-thirty when she finally got up there in front of that sympathetic, responsive, supportive audience.

The hellishness resumed when Andy, about to fold himself into the back of Joe's classic black Alfa-Romeo roadster, discovered a three-inch, shiny-new scratch low on the left rear fender. Joe, scowling, silent, drove them around the block to the garage where the car had been parked; there he climbed out, reintroduced himself to the attendant, a large shaven-headed man with one gold earring, and invited him to see the scratch. The man said he was seeing it for the first time, which Joe found hard to believe. It was after ten when Rosemary persuaded him that she really wanted to get home, and that lawyers, not threats, were the next logical step if it was really that important.

"If?" Joe said. "*If?*"

That was roughly when the water main was bursting at the intersection of Eighth Avenue and Thirty-ninth Street.

"I'm telling you, Rosie, you couldn't have been better," Joe said as they sat locked in traffic between Thirty-second and Thirty-third Streets. "You had them in the palm of your hand all the way."

"Oh please," she said. "That was the friendliest audience anybody ever spoke to. I could have"—she shook her head, waved a hand at him—"the *phone book.*"

"Go on, you were great." He buffed at the dashboard with the heel of a hand. "Wasn't she, Andy?"

"You were."

Rosemary turned around, squinted at him, sitting huddled behind them. Glints of light brushed his hair, cheekbones, beard. "Are you all right?" she asked.

He stayed silent, then said, "No, not really. I must have eaten something . . ." He moved a hand to his middle.

"Ahhh," she said, reaching over the seat, touching his other hand on his knee. "I hope it wasn't that ham-and-Swiss . . ."

"No, I don't think so," he said.

"Ham, you got to be careful," Joe said, putting a tape in the deck.

They rolled, in a slow tide of taller traffic, across Thirty-third Street and up Tenth Avenue, while Ella Fitzgerald sang the *Irving Berlin Songbook.* She was more than halfway through it when, after eleven, they were finally back on Eighth Avenue heading up through the Forties. Rosemary didn't fret unduly about Judy; she'd either be asleep on the sofa or, more likely, doing anagrams with the Scrabble tiles. *Roast Mules!* She'd have to beg her for the answer again, really literally get down on her knees and *beg* this time—just in case Judy did take off for parts unknown. Maddening, the time wasted pushing around those ten damn tiles!

"Clear sailing from here on in," Joe said.

"Bite your tongue."

"No, you." He watched in the mirror, easing to the right, slowing. A howling police car flinging red and white lights raced past them, another car following, lights flailing, the howls dropping pitch as they passed. Ella sang that as far as she was concerned, it was a lovely day, and everything was okay.

"It's a hellish night, Ella," Rosemary said, watching the police-car lights shrinking ahead.

Ella countered with, "*Isn't this a lovely day to be caught in the rain? You were going on your way, now you've got to remain—*"

"Get the news," Rosemary said.

"I like this."

"Me too," Joe said, looking in the mirror, easing right and slowing again. Rosemary jabbed at the dash, pushed buttons. "Ooh!" Joe said. "Okay. Middle button. Take it easy." An ambulance screamed past them. "Oho!" he said, smiling at her, his brows raised. "We've got our Irish up!"

She drew a breath, relaxed into the bucket seat.

A woman talked about flooded basements in Hell's Kitchen, disrupted subway service. About the fire on West Houston Street—two people dead, ten families homeless four days before Christmas.

Rosemary sighed, shook her head. Turned around as a howling police car raced past them, lights flailing. "How you doing?" she asked.

"So-so."

"Andy," she asked, her chin on her hand on the seat top, "who does Phil remind you of?"

He stayed silent.

She said, "Leah Fountain. The eyes? The chin?"

He said, "Yes, you're right."

"Uh-oh."

She turned. They were stopped for the light at Columbus

Circle; up ahead, on the left, a dazzle of lights, red-white-amber, spun-flashed-blinked at the base of the Tower. She said, "Oh God . . ."

Joe patted her coat-covered thigh. "Could be nothing," he said. Left his hand there.

Andy gave a laugh. "A bomb scare. Lutherans Against Luther."

"I'm glad you're feeling better," Rosemary said, squinting ahead against the flashing lights.

Joe took his hand from her thigh and shifted into first.

What gives?" he asked out the window.

The cop letting them through to the garage entrance crouched and said, "A murder, that's all they told me. Love you, Rosemary!"

They drove down the ramp, down the ramp, down the ramp, down the ramp. On the lower level, Joe pulled up in front of the uniformed attendant; she hurried around the car, bent, and opened Rosemary's door. "Hey, Rosemary!" she said. "You looked so cool over there!"

"Thanks," Rosemary said, climbing—with a hand from the attendant—out of the ridiculously low car. *A man his age . . .* Spotting the embroidered name, she said, "Thanks, Keesha," and pointed upstairs. "Do you know anything about—"

Keesha leaned close, brown eyes wide. "A woman been killed," she said. "In the lobby, in a boutique. Blood all over."

Rosemary drew breath.

"*Where* did you say?" Andy asked, looking up, halfway out of his berth. Rosemary gave him a hand. "A boutique," she said along with Keesha.

He stood up, frowning. Arched his back, kneading at it.

"What is it?" Joe asked, standing on the other side.

"A woman been killed," Keesha said, going around the hood of the Alfa. "In a boutique. I don't know which."

Rosemary said, "I want to get upstairs. Andy, you go right up to your place and take something and get into bed. You look awful. Do you have any Pepto-Bismol or anything like that?"

"I'll be okay," he said.

She put her hand to his forehead, held it there, looking away, frowning. He stood still, watching her. "You don't have a fever," she said, lowering her hand, looking at him, "but take a couple of aspirin anyway. Do you have tea? Make some, or order some."

"You were really good," he said. "Even a tough audience would have started thinking."

She said, "Praise from the master. *Merci.* Do what I said."

She walked with him to the AUTHORIZED PERSONNEL ONLY door, kissed his cheek as he ran his card through the lock. Joe came over and held the door open while Andy carded the elevator door and went into the red-and-brass cab, turned to them. "Thanks for the wheels, Joe baby," he said. Smiled at her as the cab closed.

"Get *him,*" Joe said, letting the outer door close. "Joe Hollywood."

Smiling, she said, "Let's call it a night, okay? I'm bushed."

"Me too," he said. They linked arms and hands, and walked toward the elevators. "Slow driving like that is murder," he said. "Wrong word."

"I wonder who she is, poor woman." She shuddered.

"We'll hear tomorrow. I wonder which boutique. Talk about shit publicity." He touched the button.

They kissed each other.

"You were great," he said.

"Thanks," she said. "And thanks for taking us. I'm sorry about the scratch."

"Thanks for reminding me."

When she came out of the elevator, Luis was at the desk, with the phone at his ear, pushing buttons, shaking his head. "I never saw anything like this before," he told her, putting the phone down, standing up. "Every line is busy. Is it true? A murder in one of the boutiques? Dogs went crazy?"

"I didn't hear *that,*" she said, "but the other . . ." She nodded. "A woman."

He crossed himself.

"Did you let Judy Kharyat in?" she asked.

"Dennis told me to," he said, "but she didn't show up."

She stood looking at him a moment, and said, "Thanks," and turned and went down the hall, getting out her card.

"Are you still expecting her?"

"*Yes!*" she called, walking faster.

She let herself in and went to the private-line phone in the living room.

Zero messages.

She picked up the phone, tapped Judy's number.

Closed her eyes, listening to the message.

Opened them. "Judy, this is Rosemary," she said. "Pick up if you're there . . . This is important. Judy? Please pick up."

She waited.

Beep, dial tone.

She hung up.

Shucked her coat off onto a chair, stood in her I ♥ ANDY sweatshirt and jeans.

Judy down there? Grabbed by some maniac on her way in?

Or was she somehow, somewhy, on one of those stalled subway trains? Or maybe—and this was a real possibility—stuck in the elevator in her own building? So Miss Punctuality was late; she could show up any second now with a standard urban horror story, especially tonight.

She turned on the local news—radio and TV both, just loud enough to hear.

Leaned against the window frame, looking down at the roofs of cars, vans, ambulance, in a swirling light show of red, white, and amber.

A truly hellish night.

13

NEW YORK City's newspaper readers, and its citizens who only glance at newsstands, relish those rare and delightful days when the two major tabloids headline the same headline. Tuesday, December 21st, was such a day, its twin front pages a true collector's item.

Not only were the identical headlines typical of the "feisty, irreverent" style that had enabled both journals to survive right up to the rim of the new century, *but also* each of the two pages tucked fire and flood into a pair of those little boxes up top *in the same order.* Different wording there, but hey, you can't expect miracles, can you?

A hideous crime, madman's work, the poor woman savaged in a way so bizarrely theatrical; and the setting, that building, that *boutique!*—a tabloid editor's dream. The headline had offered itself on a silver platter: BLOODFEST AT TIFFANY'S!

Big, black, stacked in three lines.

The reports in the two papers differed not much less. One said the dogs that smelled the still-warm blood were Weimaraners belonging to the owner of one of the upper-floor apartments; the other said they were wolfhounds belonging to the building's owner.

Both papers had the victim lying naked on the boutique's central counter, her arms at her sides—likened by one to a patient on an operating table, by the other to a sacrifice to a primitive god.

They agreed on the seven steak knives and the icepick. One said that other pieces of cutlery had been placed on and around the body; the other gave specifics. One mentioned minor looting—a few bracelets and watches, a punch bowl.

Both papers featured the same wire-service telephoto in the same tepid newsprint colors: a side view of the victim, blurred where you expected, lying on the glass counter filled with touched-up sparkling riches, festooned with ribbons of reddish blood. The silver handles of the icepick and three knives were circled in white; a few spoons and forks could be seen, and in the background, holly branches.

According to both papers, the luckless victim remained unidentified as of press time. She appeared to be in her late twenties and a Hindu; the icepick had been driven through the dime-size red dot on her forehead.

Luckless all right.

Jinxed, you might even say.

It was only when the coroner's men began readying the body for removal that someone wondered if she might possibly be Andy's Indian dish. You couldn't be sure, even the bellmen couldn't, the way she pulled the veil across her face in public most of the time, and Indian women with the dot aren't so unusual in New York City, especially in a hotel with an international clientele. But still, Andy's got a penthouse apartment and she's the right age, shouldn't somebody maybe give him a call?

When Rosemary called down to the desk at midnight to ask the night man if the woman had been identified, he told her to sit tight, Andy was on his way up.

Hellishness II. Or was it III?

Andy had been hyper, on second wind, and distraught. Beyond distraught—enraged, furious, at the lunatic killer or killers.

He filled her in on what little was known at that time. An inside job, beyond a doubt. The killer or killers had not only known how to disable the boutique's security system and fail-safe backup system, they had known the out-of-the-way location of the control box for the window shades; had known even—though this may only have been a matter of luck—that the boutique's staff had left en masse minutes after the eight o'clock closing to attend a wake for one of their number who had died that afternoon.

Questioning of building and boutique staffs, hotel guests, office workers, and apartment owners and *their* guests would begin in the morning. Thousands of people would have to be interviewed.

Rosemary wept, mourning Judy, so young, so smart, so sure of herself—except where Andy was concerned—and mourning too the wrenching fact that at the dawn of the year 2000, despite Christmas, despite Andy, despite the advent of the Lighting, a woman alone still wasn't safe in the heart of what was supposedly a civilized world capital.

Andy's outrage was naturally on a more intense and personal level. When Rosemary was finally dozing off, around three, wondering if maybe he knew what Judy had meant about reading something in April or May, she heard him on the phone in the living room describing the murder scene to someone, using phrases like *"off-the-wall lunacy"* and *"Grand Guignol horror show"*—sounding as steamed as if he had the actual killer or killers by the throat and was venting all his anger and sorrow. Good, it would help him . . .

"*. . . a production of the fucking Theatre Guild?!*"

Joe came over at nine with the tabloids and a box of doughnuts, to keep Rosemary company while Andy went with William and Polly down to City Hall to meet with the Mayor and the Police Commissioner and representatives of the media. Andy asked Muhammed to drive them so Joe could be free.

Andy had evidently been on the phone all night with GC's major backers; there was concern that if word got out that Judy, *Andy's* Judy, was the luckless victim in the crime that—thanks to its bizarre, lunatic, off-the-wall theatricality—was traveling with the sunrise around the whole world of tabloid journalism and TV, the resulting media focus on Andy and the GC inner circle in such an unsavory context the week before the Lighting might disaffect some people. Right-wing Muslims, say. The Amish. The Lighting would be ragged and incomplete, instead of the unified, transcendent communion that was its intended purpose.

Andy was confident he'd be able to persuade the Mayor and the others to keep Judy's identity under wraps till January first. They too wanted a flawless Lighting, and Christmas vacations had been planned and prepared for. William had found a tenable legal argument, in case one was needed for sweetening. Polly, the flirty widow of both a state senator and a judge in the Surrogate Court, had dirt on everybody.

Sipping black coffee from a hotel cup, Rosemary stood in her warm-but-not-warm-enough Irish wool sweater gazing down at the ten damn tiles segregated from the rest of the herd. Deservedly, the lousy little bastards. She pushed them around into LOUSETRASM.

From there into LOSTMAUSER. German soldier's problem. OUTSLAREMS. "Why seven knives?" she asked.

"When they find him, they'll ask him," Joe said, sitting on the sofa with a tabloid on a crossed leg, reading through half-glasses, an arm on the sofa back, Andy's face smiling from his sweatshirt.

Rosemary turned and paced slowly back toward the foyer, holding the cup with both hands, frowning over it.

Over his glasses, Joe watched her going by. "Sit awhile," he said.

She stopped, looked down at the other tabloid on the coffee table. Shook her head. "They think they're so clever," she said. "They're sick, disgusting *jackals* who ought to be ashamed of themselves. They're a disgrace to their profession."

"Tiffany's agrees," he said.

She paced on toward the foyer.

Turned and stopped there. "Why Tiffany's, really?" she asked him. "Prime location, heaviest traffic, best likelihood of passing hound dogs. Why not one of the smaller boutiques on the other side? Why a boutique at all, in fact?"

"Sweetheart," he said, turning a page, "we don't ask reasonable questions of this kind of pervert. Or per*verts.*" He sighed, read on through the glasses.

She paced slowly back toward the Scrabble table, sipping, frowning.

Stopped in the center of the room.

He looked at her.

She turned to him. "Was there anything else," she asked, "besides the knives and the—pick?"

"Uh-huh," he said. "Forks and spoons in the pictures. Wait a minute . . ." He leafed back through the tabloid's pages, licked a finger.

She moved closer, watching him with dark-ringed eyes. Put the cup down, raked a hand through her hair.

He mumbled down a column, said, " 'He also said that *other pieces of cutlery were placed on and around the victim.*'"

"What others? How many?" she asked.

"Doesn't say."

"Maybe the *Times* has it . . ." She looked around.

"Save your energy," he said. "It's on Z-nineteen, 'Woman Slain in Boutique.' That's about it."

"Check that one," she said.

He put his tabloid aside, lowering his leg, and leaned toward her, elbows on knees, Andy smiling at her on his sweatshirt. "Rosie," he said, "Judy is dead. How many spoons were around doesn't *mean* anything. These guys have their *things*, their fetishes; they need things to be certain ways. Please, honey, don't dwell on it. It won't do any good."

"Will you please look," she said. "I don't want to touch the rag."

He sighed and picked up the other tabloid. "Myself, I think it's catchy," he said, opening it.

"You would," she said. Waited.

"Son of a gun," he said, "they've even got the pattern, 'Edwardian.' Eleven each, spoons and forks."

"Eleven," she said. Stood still a moment. Turned and headed toward the table.

He watched her.

She messed OUTSLAREMS up, pushed the tiles around a

moment—and stood looking out the window, tapping a tile against the thumbnail of her other hand. "Do you by any chance know her middle name?" she asked.

"Judy's?" he said.

She turned, nodded.

"I don't even know if she had one," he said. "And would you please tell me what *that's* got to do with anything?"

She said, "There's a phone book in the drawer in there. Maybe there's a middle initial, that's what matters. Kharyat— K, H, A, R, Y, A, T. West End Avenue."

"Her middle initial matters," he said, looking at her.

She nodded. "Crucially," she said.

He sighed, opened a drawer between his feet, lifted out the thick Manhattan phone book in a burgundy binder. "Why do I suddenly feel like Dr. Watson?" he asked.

She waited.

He found the K's, leafed; she watched him, her thumb rubbing the tile.

"It's the only one," he said, a hand at his glasses. "Kharyat, J. S."

She reached over the roses, spread her fingers; he caught the tile, looked at it, at her. "How'd you do it?" he asked.

"I'm a psychic," she said. "I have visions."

She turned and walked across the room. Stood looking at Andy della Robbia leaning on his easel atop the TV—seeing and being seen.

She turned around and said, "Eleven spoons."

Joe looked at her, holding a white arc of doughnut, his mouth full.

"Eleven forks," she said. "Seven steak knives." Drew breath. "One icepick. What are they?"

He swallowed. Said, "What *are* they?"

"In Tiffany's," she said.

"They're something different somewhere else?" he asked.

"Maybe," she said. "Somewhere else they could be stainless steel, or aluminum. In Tiffany's they're silver." She raked both hands back through her hair, clutched it. "Thirty pieces," she said, dark-ringed eyes staring at him. "Thirty pieces of silver."

His mouth opened, crumbs dropping.

She stepped closer to him. "Thirty pieces of silver," she said, "in and on the body—of Judith S. Kharyat."

He blinked at her, putting the doughnut down.

She stepped closer. "Judith S. Kharyat." Leaned over the roses and rushed it: "Judithesskharyat."

"*Judas Iscariot?*" he asked.

She nodded.

They stared at each other.

"I have a feeling," she said, "it's not the name she was born with." She stood straight. Closed her eyes, put a hand across her forehead, turned. Started pacing a slow, wide circle . . .

Watching her, he said, "Do you? Have visions?"

"Sometimes," she said, pacing, holding her forehead, eyes closed.

He watched her, backhanding his mouth.

She stopped and faced him, drew breath. "She needed a name that sounded Indian," she said. "Vassar-Indian—for when she got noticeably un-Hindu, I guess. She was a smart one, God bless her. And she likes, *liked* word games and puzzles." She stood a moment, blinking, lips tight, hands clasped tight together. "She came on to Andy," she said, "planning to dig up dirt on him and GC, to expose it as a scam, and him as, I don't know, a con man, a charlatan. We all know who *he* looks like, so she called herself Judith S. Kharyat, Judy Kharyat. She must have figured it would sail right past everybody, which it did, and she probably didn't plan to be here for more than a month or so anyway, if that. But Andy cast his magic spell"—she cleared her throat—"and she fell in love with him. She was stuck with the role. He 'derailed' her, she said. I should have made the connection right then."

"Made *what* connection?" Joe asked, peering at her.

"I'll bet you anything you want," she said, bending, choosing a doughnut, "that she was really Alice Rosenbaum. It's a perfect interlock. The medical examiner, or whoever is doing the autopsy, ought to know by now."

"What are you *talking* about?" Joe asked. "Who's Alice *Rosenbaum?* I never even *heard* the name before!"

"You probably did a few years ago and forgot," Rosemary said, eating a doughnut, holding her elbow. "I heard it in a PBS docu I watched a couple of weeks ago. One of my brothers dated an Alice Rosenbaum in high school and had fights with my father about it, so I noticed the name. The PBS Alice Rosenbaum was the female member of the Ayn Rand Brigade, the woman at the throttle of that train they hijacked. I guess trains were significant for her. Using 'derailed,' I mean."

Joe said, "*Judy* is—was that PA?"

Rosemary nodded. "I'm sure," she said. "It *has* to be." She ate some more. "The name can't be real," she said, "and no other woman would have had to do the Indian bit in the first place."

"What do you mean, I don't *get* it," Joe said, standing up. "She *had* to be an Indian? Why? Why wouldn't a wig and glasses and Alice J.—Smith or Jones have been enough?"

Rosemary tapped a fingertip at the center of her forehead. "Her tattoo," she said. "They have tattoos on their foreheads! What was she going to do, wear a band-aid for a month? Count on covermark? *She needed the dot to hide the dollar sign.*"

Joe stared openmouthed at her.

She finished the doughnut, brushed sugar from her lips and fingers, licked them.

He held his forehead, shaking his head. "Jeez, I'm all at sea here," he said. "So whoever—gave her the thirty pieces of silver"—he lowered his hand, looking at her—"was saying that that's what she was, a Judas? Betraying Andy?"

She turned away.

"*How?*" Joe asked. "She loved him, like you said. Sure, you could see they had a little tiff or something last week, but there's no way *he* could have—if you could even *imagine* such a—He was with *us* the whole time!"

She turned around, aimed her dark-ringed eyes at him. "The others weren't," she said. The buzzer buzzed, Andy's buzz.

They stayed looking at each other a moment, and she let breath out and walked away, slowing as she reached the foyer—Andy buzzed again—slowing more as she neared the door. She stood a moment. Joe moved out from behind the coffee table, watching.

She opened the door.

Andy nodded. "Mission accomplished," he said.

"Oh good," she said.

They hugged each other; he said "How you doing," kissing her temple, smoothing her hair back.

"Okay," she said. Kissed his cheek. "You're back so soon!"

His eyes shone. "Wait!" he said, closing the door behind him. They went arm in arm into the living room. "Joe!" he said.

"Andy . . ." Joe said, looking at him.

"Sit down, both of you," he said, taking his arm from around her. "I'm going to tell you something that's going to absolutely knock your socks off." He unzipped his jacket.

They looked at each other.

"I mean it," he said, shedding the jacket, looking back and forth between them. "Sit down or fall down, take your choice." He straightened his sweatshirt—navy, no message.

Joe said, "Is this maybe about a tattoo?"

Andy stared at him. Swallowed. "Who called?" he asked. "I've got to know who leaked it."

"Your mother figured it out," Joe said, nodding at her.

Andy turned and stared. "*That Judy was Alice Rosenbaum?*"

Rosemary nodded.

"*How?*"

Looking at him, she said, "The thirty pieces of silver, and the name."

"The *name?*" he said.

She said, "Judith S. Kharyat . . ."

"Say it fast," Joe said.

Andy's lips moved. He stared—at her, at him—and clapped the side of his head. "They even thought of *that!*" he said. "A name that reinforces everything! I never put it together! She told me her middle name was this long Indian . . ." He spun a hand, looking at Rosemary. Stopped the hand. "Don't you see who did it?" he asked. "Don't you see who's behind it all?"

She said, looking at him, "No . . ."

He turned to Joe.

Joe shook his head, looking at him.

"The rest of the Brigade!" he said. "The five guys! Or some of them. The Commish got word who she was just as we got there. I realized right away what the story was, what it meant: they had planted her here to spy on us, they were getting even with her for—I guess you'd say switching teams—and *at the same time* they were messing up *the Lighting* by making it look as if she was killed for betraying *me* somehow! Because I look the way I do, and the thirty pieces of silver—which that *name* only reinforces! That's why they killed her in such an attention-getting way. Really, who except someone looking for absolute maximum worldwide publicity would—I *mean*, Tiffany's, nudity, blood, silver—come *on*, it *had* to be a set-up."

Joe, gasping, said, "Whew, kiddo, I have to admit, your mother and I had a little nervous moment there, at least I did, I shouldn't speak for you, Rosie. What a *relief.* Whew!" He wagged a hand, slapped at his chest.

Rosemary said, "It sounds logical . . ."

Andy lifted a finger. "But before I could even say a *word,*" he said, "the Mayor had put the whole thing together himself! Including the thirty pieces of silver!" He tapped his temple, nodding. "Once he laid it all out, everyone agreed in a flash. She stays unidentified, both identities, till after the Lighting, after vacation, Jan third. The FBI is mounting full surveillance on Fort Whatever-they-call-it in Montana, and their computer already found a connection between one of the Brigade members and a lawyer on the eighteenth floor."

"What a relief," Joe said, checking the doughnuts.

Andy turned to Rosemary, took her by the shoulders. He sighed, gazing into her eyes. "At least we know who did it," he said. "I hope that helps a *little.*"

Nodding at him, she said, "It does, dear."

"Ahh, poor baby . . ." He kissed her nose, hugged her. "You look old enough to be my mother." She punched, he chuckled.

Joe, eating as he watched them, smiled.

Rosemary, looking up at Andy, said, "It really *does* help, angel. I'd probably have seen myself that the Brigade was behind it if I'd had more time to think about it. I only realized who she was minutes before you came in. I'm glad the FBI is on it so quickly; I'm sure they'll find them." She smiled up at him—radiating candor and sincerity. And honesty and openness.

The Antijudas . . .
     It figured she'd have been in there among his twelve antiapostles.

Eleven now.

She split MULTAROSES, shifted the tiles, made ASTROLUMES.

Sitting at the table in the late afternoon, after a nap and a shower. Soft lounging pajamas, soft jazz on the radio, soft snow sifting down past the window.

ULTRAMESSO. Like a teenager's room. Not so common a word, though, that five- and six-year-olds use it.

Could Judy/Alice have been lying about Roast Mules too—to drive her bats? Was there really *no* word using those ten letters? Was it a hoax, like her saris and the dot?

No . . . Not even a PA would do *that* . . .

And they'd been friends. That hadn't been a hoax.

MORTUALESS . . .

Hutch had been stopped from telling her Roman's real identity by the spell Roman and his coven cast, the spell that finally killed him.

Judy had been stopped from telling her—what? That Andy had a coven? Were witchcraft and Satanism, not fraud and tax evasion, what Alice Rosenbaum had found—what Andy had derailed her into? And after she had told *her*, who would the Antijudas have told today? The *Times*? The tabloids? They'd sit on *that* for about two seconds, coming from her. Or a publisher, for a book to be published next April or May? Why else would she have been killed that way? They must have been high on something, like many a knife-wielding murderer in recent history—far fewer nowadays, thanks to Andy.

Could the Antijudas have spread the worse news, the Bad News?

No. If she had known who Andy's father was, she would never have opened up to his mother, not even partially—and would have pried for more information besides. The Indian cultural thing—ha!—would have given her the excuse.

Which meant, probably, that the eleven others didn't know either. Coven members shared their secret knowledge; that was one of Roman's lures, whenever he tried to get her to join . . .

STEALORMUS . . .

Last Christmas Eve—*her* last, six months ago—she had let Andy go to Minnie and Roman's alone, for the first time, and stay overnight. He had been five and a half, to the day. There were rituals that had to be performed half a year before his next birthday, Roman said, instructions to be given. They were honoring their part of the bargain; she had to honor hers. His father had rights too. Rites too.

She needed the coven. When you have a toddler with beautiful tiger eyes, and horn buds slightly less beautiful, and other parts even less beautiful—all of which today he presumably controlled (she wasn't asking) by the same semi-Satanic willpower that gave him hazel eyes—when you have a toddler like that, you can't drop him off at a preschool and go on to the job. When you really desperately need a sitter for a few hours, you can't call an agency or the teenager in the apartment down the hall.

The coven paid the bills. The women were doting nanas on whom she relied only when absolutely necessary, under strict rules whose following she checked in secret ways. All of

them, men and women—except Laura-Louise, the bitch—
treated her with the same helpfulness and respect everybody
gave her today.

Roman promised her—he made a vow he said was sacred
to him—that Andy wouldn't be harmed in any way or pressed
to do anything he resisted, that he would only be strengthened
mentally and physically in ways that would be useful to him all
his life. The experience would be inspiring and uplifting, like
any other good religious service. Though she couldn't be there as
an onlooker, she was more than welcome, as she surely knew by
now, as a celebrant. The coven could certainly use some young
blood—his old eyes twinkled—and there were two places empty.
That way she could keep an eye on Andy.

Thanks but no thanks.

She had spent half that Christmas Eve sitting on a footstool
in a deshelved closet whose back opened, when it wasn't bolted
on the other side as it was then, into a closet next door—the
same passage she'd been carried through that night in October of '65. Sitting there with an ear to the bottom of a glass
pressed to white-painted plywood, she heard faintly now and
then echoes of the piping flute of that night, the chanting, the
beating drum. The tang of tannis root sneaked through cracks,
sour but not unpleasant . . . A whiff of sulfur, though, sickened
her. Had *he* come up, or out, or materialized from outer space
or wherever the hell?

She wept for Andy then. She should have taken him and
run. She *would*, and before his birthday—far, to San Francisco
or Seattle. She'd get the plane fare somehow, and find an agency
or children's hospital, a church-run hospital, that would help her.

Once the sulfur smell was gone and there was just the scent
of tannis again, stronger soon in the closet's shelter, she felt better.
She recalled the tannis taste of the drinks Minnie had made

for her during her pregnancy, drinks that had nourished Andy. Minnie and Roman *loved* him, they'd take good care of him.

Later she poured herself a glass of eggnog, added a splash of bourbon, and watched *It's a Wonderful Life*—on the way to becoming a TV Christmas tradition. Sweet movie. Second time she'd seen it.

When Andy came through the closets the next morning, he was fine, happy, glad to see-hug-kiss her and run into the living room. Had he had a good time? He nodded, looking up at the tree. "What did you do?" she asked, kneeling beside him, smiling at the lights shining in his eyes, on his cheeks.

"I said I wouldn't tell," he said. "Should I?"

Her hand on his flannel-shirted back, she said, "If you really didn't want to say it, yes. Or if you changed your mind and want to tell me anyway. Kids can do that. If you don't want to, no. I gave permission, I said you could go."

He chose not to tell.

Her last Christmas. He'd had twenty-seven since, or this would be the twenty-seventh. The ones when he was growing up and in his teens, at least, must have been like that one, scented with tannis, caroled by whining flutes and chanting. Black Christmases . . .

TREMULOSSA . . .

He had told her he was through with Satanism—after looking her in the eye and saying he would never lie to her again. If he *had* lied . . . Friday night could be just the time to find out.

He had said on the plane that he and Judy had plans for Christmas Eve, that they would exchange presents with her and Joe on Christmas Day in the morning. And Judy had started saying something the first time they played Scrabble about goings-on on the ninth floor . . .

Not a bad space—the amphitheater and its dressing rooms

and green room, the conference rooms, all carpeted, sound-proofed by floors of empty offices above and below—not a bad space at all for a Black Mass. Better than Minnie and Roman's living room, for sure.

Five people to get it spick-and-span? Didn't the cleaning crew hit nine? Ultramesso?

SOULMASTER . . .

Snow strummed the window, falling faster now, windswept swaths of white, whipping down out of darkening sky. Score one for the forecasters; four inches by midnight, they had said, two to four more by morning. Wind gusts up to forty miles an hour.

Snow was probably coming down at the radio station too; Bing Crosby had begun dreaming of a white Christmas.

Just like the ones he used to know.

THREE

14

THE BLIZZARD of '99, lasting two and a half days and dumping two to five feet of the white stuff all the way up the Eastern seaboard from Cape Hatteras to Cape Cod, was far and away the peak, the pinnacle, the Everest of the century's blizzards, and the paramount headache of them all.

New York City was lucky, only 23.8 inches. God got thanks for that—Boston, it was said, would *never* dig out—and "Mother Nature" (God in drag?) took the rap for the rest of it: the buried commuter trains, the collapsed roofs of supermarkets, the empty theaters and stores, the stranded travelers, the homebound everyone else except children with sleds and cross-country skiers.

The last flakes fell and the sun came out early Friday morning, as if in direct obedience to the feisty, irreverent order of only one of the tabloids: STUFF IT, BING. Midtown Manhattan was a grid of lumped tundras where people tramped, kicked, skied, threw snowballs, frisked with dogs, pulled children on plastic shells—while store managers watched, smiling, from open doorways.

Tiffany's alone was jammed with card-waving customers, not only the Fifth Avenue store and its satellite boutiques but the branches in White Plains and Short Hills as well—proof yet again that as long as they spell the name right, there's no such thing as bad publicity.

"Hi. Let's go look at the tree."

They hadn't seen or spoken to each other since Tuesday morning, when her obviously wretched state of exhaustion had given her a legitimate excuse to send him and Joe on their way, each with a kiss on the cheek, Joe with the rest of the doughnuts and both the rags, thank you. Andy had said he was going to the retreat but would be back in time for Christmas-morning brunch.

She had been glad of his going—the radiating hadn't been exactly a lark—but she had wondered whether it was grief or guilt or a mixture of both that he was retreating from, and in whose company, if anyone's. She imagined him or them in an adobe-and-steer-horn *Playboy* pad surrounded by desert. Another subject left unmentioned; a retreat is a retreat.

"You there?"

"Yes," she said, moving with the phone to the bedroom window. "Where are you?"

"Forty-five floors overhead. Just got in."

"*How?*" she asked, looking down at the billowed white quilt laid over the park.

"Plane, chopper, and subway. Feel like some exercise? The snow's more or less packed in the middle of the streets and the plows are getting plowed out. It's real Christmasy."

She sighed, and said, "We had a tree of our own the last

Christmas I remember. You were five and a half, we trimmed it together. Do you remember that?"

"Completely forgot it. That's why I'm still in Arizona. Do you have boots? The boutiques must be sold out."

"I've got," she said.

Everybody had—boots brown, black, red, yellow. Gloves, mittens, scarves, hats, earlaps, red cheeks (those usually pinkish), I ♥ ANDY buttons, I ♥ ROSEMARY buttons, big smiles, shiny shades or eyes smiling right back at you.

"The city's never better than after a big snow," Rosemary said, pluming out breath, tramping along arm in arm with Andy down the center of Central Park South amid dozens of other proud Reclaimers of the Land from Vehicles. "It really brings out the best in people."

"I guess it does," Andy said, as they paused at Seventh Avenue to watch some men, women, and children helping a crew of sanitation workers dig out a drifted-over salt spreader. Another group farther down the avenue was doing similar work on something else large and orange.

They tramped on down Central Park South among the other pioneers, steadying each other now and then; the 23.8 inches wasn't packed down hard yet.

Rosemary was well Garboed: new bigger shades, a scarf around her head, the floppy-brimmed hat, and a coat out of *Ninotchka*—worn maybe by a Russian colonel. She had been on the verge of giving it to a bellman.

Andy's simple street disguise had never failed him: shades and a jumbo I ♥ ANDY button—transforming him instantly into one of the city's, the planet's, legions of Andy wannabes.

One of the better ones. A cop in shades coming toward them gave him a gloved thumb up. "Yo, Andy!" he grinned. "Great! *Numero uno!*"

They smiled back at him. Andy said, "Thanks, love ya," as they passed.

"The voice too!" the cop cried, pointing, walking backward. "Say something else!"

"Up yours!"

The cop laughed, waved.

Rosemary elbowed. "*Andy,*" she said.

"It's part of the disguise!" he said. "Would Andy say that? Never!"

"Ohh . . ."

"Say shit, it'll help."

They laughed—"*Shit!*"—following a right-turning packed-down trail into Sixth Avenue. There the Land had been Reclaimed as far as the eye could see—white tundra dotted with people, bordered with car-shaped igloos.

"When did they give up on 'Avenue of the Americas'?" Rosemary asked, looking up at a street sign.

"Officially, just a few months ago," Andy said.

Smiling, she said, "Hutch used to say someday they'd count the syllables."

The name cast a pall.

She had told him about Hutch, the friend he had been to her, that Roman's coven had killed him.

They tramped down the Sixth Avenue tundra, holding gloved hands, scanning their shades about, smiling.

Pausing in mid-avenue, they watched a few people scooping snowdrifts from a skewed limo with partly uncovered windows.

Andy pitched in. Rosemary too. When an unlocked door was found and opened, no one was inside.

They waved and tramped on, brushing snow from their fronts.

On the West Fifty-first Street tundra they tramped past the red-neoned rear marquee of Radio City Music Hall. Rosemary said, "When are you going to do your next live show? I can't wait to see one."

Andy drew breath; plumed it from his nostrils. He said, "I don't think I'm going to be doing any more, not for a while anyway."

"Why not?" she asked. "They're terrifically effective. The woman at the nursing home who told me about you, she saw you here and talked about it as if—she'd had a religious experience."

Turning his shades from her, he said, "I don't know, I just sort of feel that after the Lighting I ought to take a little time off and—reevaluate what I want to do next."

She said, "I've been doing some work on a presentation for a talk show. I don't want to just come in and say, 'I'm here, I'm Andy's Mom, take me.' I've got a great name for it, you gave it to me. 'Fresh Eyes.' Isn't that a good name for a program dealing with the differences between now and then?"

"Yeah, it is," he said.

She said, "I want to deal with big things, like the mistake of talking the terrorists' language, and little things, like rollerblades—with people connected somehow with whatever the area is."

"Don't forget we're going away for a while," he said.

She blew out a long plume. "No," she said. "No, I really don't think that's a good idea. Not right now."

He drew breath, clamped his lips.

They tramped along in their shades, gloved hands joined.

Turned right into Rockefeller Plaza and froze, cowering.

"Wow!" Andy said, raising his free hand. Rosemary whistled. People moved around and past them in both directions.

They made their way closer to the towering cone of multi-colored lights. Rosemary said, "I'll tell you one thing fresh eyes see right off the bat: too much! It used to be you could see there was a *tree* holding everything up; that's just a gigantic cone of lights and baubles. It could have styrofoam inside it."

"Actually they cut back from last year," Andy said. "People started complaining."

They made their way closer—on almost-clear asphalt, in a crowd, between walls of plowed-back snow.

"*But,*" she said, when they had found a vantage point where they could stand and see the tree and the skaters on the rink before it, "if you're going to go for glitz . . ."

He nodded, looking up at the tree.

She looked at him, at the lights shining on his shades, on his cheeks above his beard.

"Say hello to Andy," a man before them said, tugging the mitten of a boy of seven or so. The boy nibbled his other mitten, looking up at Andy. The man winked at them.

Rosemary said, "Be nice . . ."

Andy crouched down, smiled at the boy, took his shades off, said, "Hi."

The boy got his mitten down to his chin and said, "Are you really Andy?"

"To be perfectly honest," Andy said, "at the moment I'm not sure. Who are you?"

"James," the boy said.

"Hi, James," Andy said, offering his gloved hand.

James shook it with his mitten, said "Hi . . ." Andy said, "It's fun when there's all this snow, isn't it?"

"Yes," James said, nodding. "We're going to make a snowman."

Andy clasped his shoulder, smiled, and said, "Enjoy it, Jimbo."

He stood up. "Great kid," he said to the man, putting the shades back on.

"You," the man said, poking him in the chest, "are a ten-times-better Andy than the guy in the miniseries. And your voice is closer too."

"Years of practice," Andy said. Rosemary tugged his sleeve.

"Merry Christmas," the man said. Nodded it to her too as he steered James away toward the tree.

"Merry Christmas!" Rosemary said.

Andy waved; James waved back.

They tramped over to Seventh Avenue, a tundra being carved away by a phalanx of snowplows, and up to the Stage Deli—half empty.

"Your brother's in the corner," the waiter said, standing at the table with pad and pencil. Andy looked; another Andy waved at him. He waved back. Rosemary waved too. So did the other Andy's tablemate, Marilyn Monroe. "What'll it be?" the waiter asked.

Pastrami sandwiches, beer.

Andy chewed, shades facing the window.

Taking hers off, looking at him, Rosemary said, "Do you want to talk, Andy?"

He stayed silent a moment. Sighed, shrugged. "It's just ironic, that's all," he said, shades turning toward the half sandwich on his plate. He picked at it. "I finally find a smart, sexy woman who really prefers total darkness," he said, "and it's because it saves her from having to keep an all-over suntan. She told me Indian women never let a man see *anything*. Who knows, maybe it's true."

"I doubt it," she said. "They're very open—I *think*."

"It sure frees up the imagination," he said.

Putting on her shades, scanning, she said, "I can't eat all of this, I'm going to have them wrap it."

Central Park South had been plowed and was getting a second go; a few cars and taxis crept through a foot-thick dry mash of dirtied snow. Rosemary walked single file after Andy beside a wall of shiny snowbank.

"What are you doing tonight?"

She said, "There's an eight-thirty Mass at Saint Pat's. Joe got us seats." She walked along behind him. "What are you doing?" she asked.

"Turning in early. The trip took a lot out of me. It was worth it though."

A mailman gave him a hand over chopped-out snow steps, and they both helped Rosemary. They thanked him. "Real good," he said.

"Thanks, love ya."

"Great!"

They walked to the Tower's marquee, nodded to the winking doorman, and first she and then he passed through a revolving door into the crowded lobby of the grand hotel, its marble reaches decked with green branches and gold leaves, "Greensleeves" tintinnabu-lating overhead on medieval strings. They maneuvered between bellmen with luggage, past the desk where a sheikh and his entourage dallied, through an entanglement of French schoolgirls in uniform and a stumbling waiter spilling a bowl of oranges in their path, to the bank of elevators. "I have to pick up a few things in the drugstore,"

Rosemary said. "Sure you don't want it?" She held up the deli bag.

"Positive," Andy said, kicking an orange aside. "Around eleven tomorrow?"

"Fine," she said.

"I'll call you."

Their shades clacked as they kissed cheeks. "Merry Christmas," they said to each other, their lips smiling.

He headed for the corner beyond the elevators.

She went into the drugstore. French schoolgirls jabbered over the magazine rack, the perfume and costume-jewelry displays.

She picked up toothpaste and a flashlight, charged them to the suite, then went to the back and spoke to the smiling pharmacist. He withdrew from the counter.

Rosemary scanned the store with her shades, took them off, smiled at the clerk smiling at her. The clerk screwed a finger in her ear, wincing, as the schoolgirls hurried out the door.

The pharmacist came back, reached over the counter. "Midnight Mass?"

"You guessed it, Al. Thank you. Merry Christmas."

"A half will keep you wide awake for three or four hours. Merry Christmas, Rosemary."

"**H**i, Rosemary. Joe. Give me a call when you get in, will you? I've got a problem."

The problem, he told her when she called him, involved Mary Elizabeth, his twenty-three-year-old daughter, who had just come out as a lesbian and moved in with her lover, a woman in her forties. "Ronnie got a sudden impulse and invited them for dinner, she's big on Christmas spirit, and they're coming. The trains are getting through, and I'm afraid if I don't go, Mary Elizabeth is liable to think I'm shutting the—"

"Oh go, Joe!" she said. "Do, don't worry! I'm glad you're all sitting down together."

"And I want to meet her. I mean, if she's *living* with her, I at least want to get some kind of—"

"Joe, I'll tell you the truth," Rosemary said, "I'd just as soon go by myself. Honestly. I haven't been to church in a long time, even before the coma, and maybe it'll be better for me if it's more—private. Don't worry, go. You should, I want you to."

"Thanks, Rosie. Go in by the entrance on Fifty-first near Madison. Someone'll be there with a list, just give my name. What time tomorrow?"

"Around eleven," she said.

"See you then. Thanks again."

She was doubly thankful too, because they all were sitting down together and because she really did want to be alone. Garboing on the inside too.

She hadn't thought of going to Mass till Tuesday night, after she had decided where she'd be going later Christmas Eve. The cathedral would be packed, even though extra Masses had been scheduled this Christmas of 1999, and she didn't like the idea of wearing shades in church, so she had asked Joe if he could arrange for special seating. She had invited him because she'd had to; she sensed that he had accepted likewise. He was no more devout than she, both with their divorces.

And she'd have had to ditch him later anyway—another letdown for him.

Poor Joe. Poor both of them. He'd checked out fine and had

seen as little reason for postponing things as she did, but every time they had planned a proper night or weekend together, something had come up to get in the way. First the Dublin power failure, then the fire in the inn outside Belfast, then his pinched spinal nerve, and then the blizzard.

It was almost as if, somewhere in the universe, a malevolent spiritual power had made it his sole goal to oppose their getting into the sack together before New Year's Eve.

S he called her brothers and sister. Gave out the last of the staff Christmas gifts.

Her gifts for the GC inner circle, possibly Andy's coven—innocent until proven guilty—would wait till tomorrow or never, depending.

Judy's scarf in its Hermès wrap—she wasn't sure what she'd do with that. Wear it herself probably. An Indian design. Ha.

She ate the other half of the pastrami sandwich sitting at the window, thinking how she would put things, marshaling her thoughts so she wouldn't waste His time, assuming . . . It was, after all, one of His busier nights.

Hutch's bones must hâve been rolling over in the "worm cafeteria," as he called it.

Judy/Alice would have been annoyed too, for sure, though she probably would have accepted it as a kind of "centering" thing.

When you have proof positive, gained in a hard way, of Satan's reality—you tend to regain your belief in God's. Of course *He* may no longer believe in *you*, may even get edgy if you set foot in His house or dare to take His Holy Communion, so you maintain a respectful distance . . .

Until it seems really necessary to clarify things.

She left the Tower at seven, fully Garboed. The doorman said there were taxis around but she had allowed plenty of time, the night was clear, and she was from Nebraska; she walked.

The same route she had walked with Andy—on shoveled sidewalks now, by ranges of snow mountains pocked here and there with glints of entombed chrome.

Santas in phony beards rang their bells over their kettles—going right up there with Chanel No. 5 and Stage Deli's pastrami sandwiches on Fresh Eyes' list of Unchanged Good Things, an idea for the fourth or fifth program, or maybe a weekly feature.

She passed the entrance to Rockefeller Plaza with just a glance at the cone of night-bright lights—not too bad—and went on to Fifth Avenue, where snow mountains had been banished and traffic, what little there was, diverted. St. Patrick's Cathedral stood on the other side of the avenue in all its Gothic majesty, every detail of its tri-arched front and twin spires lavished with white frosting, brilliantly floodlighted, never more splendid.

Another big plus for 1999 New York—night lighting of landmark buildings.

She was more than an hour early. The line, behind blue police barriers, snaked around into Fiftieth Street but wasn't long enough yet to fill the pews. Travel conditions were probably keeping away a lot of people from Long Island, Westchester, all the suburbs.

The idea of house seats for serious prayer hadn't sat well with her from the beginning, and when she crossed the avenue and got a good look at some of the people in the line—bikers in studded leather, a girl with purple hair, for pete's sake—she decided to go in with the commoners; the Garbo gear wouldn't raise an eyebrow, certainly not His.

The elderly couple in front of her—they'd made it in from Westchester—smiled at her and faced forward.

The blizzard didn't start up again when she passed through the portal and vestibule; nor did lightning strike when she knelt and crossed herself. She found more than enough space in a back pew on the right, slipped in and sat.

She took a deep breath, and loosed her coat's belt and buttons. Sank back in the creaking pew, savoring the organ's cascading harmonies, marveling at the beauty and vastness of the vaulted space before her—the ranks of soaring stone pillars and arches, each pillar hung with a red-ribboned wreath, each outer arch framing stained glass that gleamed jewel-bright in the light from outside. Flats of orange candle flames flickered at the rows of side altars in their alcoves; the gold-and-white high altar and sanctuary far ahead stood empty, waiting, spotlighted, banked with masses of red poinsettias.

Throat clearing. A woman waited by the pew—stout and white-haired in a pink hat and suit, I ♥ ANDY and I ♥ ROSEMARY side by side on a shoulder. Rosemary smiled at her and slid farther toward the man on her right. The woman hesitated, smiled, squeezed herself down in. The pew creaked. "They all creak," she whispered.

"I know," Rosemary whispered.

"Merry Christmas," the woman whispered.

"Merry Christmas," Rosemary whispered.

They faced front.

The woman shifted. Folded her coat on her knees, shifted. Fussed with her handbag. Shifted. Poor dear comes to Mass and finds herself next to this weirdo in space goggles. Too embarrassed or polite to get up and look for another seat, if there is one.

Rosemary leaned toward her, tapped the stem of the shades. "Eye surgery," she whispered.

"Ah!" the woman whispered, nodding. "I *see*, I see, I was wond'rin'. What was it, dear? I'm a nurse at Saint Clare's."

Rosemary whispered. "A detached retina."

"Ahh," the nurse whispered, nodding. Patted Rosemary's hand.

They smiled at each other, faced front.

Lying in church. To an Irish nurse. Off to a great start.

She straightened her back.

Tried to get her head straight too.

The organ poured descending scales in all its voices. Almost everyone now knelt praying—the old man on her right, and the nurse too, murmuring, her broad back bent. What a lot of voices rising upward!

Rosemary eased her knees down onto the padded red leather kneeler, tucked her booted feet back under, folded her hands on the oak rim of the pew before her, lowered her head.

Sneaked the shades off and into a pocket, folded her hands again, closed her eyes, let breath out. She'd forgotten the comfort of the position. Breathed again . . .

Father, forgive me for I have sinned. As well You know. But I'm here about Andy, and about what's going on. Thank You for allowing me in. I know this is presumptuous, I guess it's from everyone talking about my miraculous awakening and my miraculous recovery so much, but I've begun to think the last few days that maybe You had a hand in Stan Shand dying when he did, so I would wake up and do something You want to be done. The problem is, I'm not sure what it is, and I'm afraid it may involve hurting Andy, maybe severely.

The pew she leaned on trembled, creaked. She waited, head bowed, while the people there reordered themselves.

I'm trying to take things a step at a time. If I find what I'm afraid I'll find tonight, Andy conducting a Black Mass, please help me take the next right step. Some kind of sign would be greatly appreciated. Is desperately needed, in fact. All I presume to ask in return is that You remember that Andy is half human— more than half, I hope—and that if things turn out badly for him, I pray You'll show him at least half of Your usual mercy. That's—

Like a steel wheel thrown through the cathedral, a scream sheared up to the vaulted ceiling, banged off into the transepts, rang back doubled into the nave, another scream shearing after it, scream after steel-wheel scream banging, ringing, shearing away echoes. Heads up, eyes up, in every pew of the cross-shaped church—nave, apse, transepts—lips bitten, rosaries kissed, hands sketching crosses.

The nurse shoved her coat and bag down between them, grabbed the pew in front, hoisted herself, squeezed out, hurried down the aisle. A few pews ahead a standing man sidled—"I'm a doctor, excuse me."

Small screams shimmered away. Silence spread, stuffed the cathedral to its walls and windows.

Sobbing down front where the nurse and others flocked. A priest hurrying out from behind the altar.

The organ poured music; everyone breathed. Prayed, whispered.

Rosemary sat straight and still, her fist at her chest where her cross had ended.

Clear enough sign, Fresh Eyes?

She swallowed, drew breath.

Gathering her coat around her, she pushed the nurse's things into the corner; got out of the pew and headed for the vestibule, belting the coat, putting on the shades, tugging down the hat as she hurried through.

"That was Rosemary! I swear it was!"

"Go *on*. Dressed like that? Leaving now? Alone? Yeah, sure, it was Rosemary."

15

SHEER COINCIDENCE, she told herself, walking along with her head down and her hands in her pockets, on the clear-swept sidewalks of Central Park South. Coincidences happen, even in St. Patrick's on Christmas Eve. Stupid of her to take some poor soul's seizure as a sign to *her* from *Him*.

Not just stupid, arrogant—casting herself as God's agent on Earth. And thinking for even an instant that, out of the hundreds of millions of prayers rising up to Him that night, He had zeroed in on hers for His immediate attention and splashy reply.

She passed hotels and apartment houses, people leaving, people arriving, Christmas gifts and Christmas grins. She walked from the heated downdraft of a broad marquee to Sixth Avenue's cold crosswind.

The Tower, nearing, shone as in daylight, the city's night-glow magnified by the snow in the park and streets. She had hoped to spot a telltale lighted window on one of GC's floors, had left a marker in her bedroom window—a blue kerchief pinned taut between the draperies, a shadeless lamp behind it—to locate the floors above. She couldn't even spot the blue window in the shiny gold-mirror facade.

When she had crossed Central Park South at Columbus Circle, she stepped to the side of the trodden snow path and looked all the way up, lowering her shades. The skyscraper, towering over her, kept its shades in place; there was no seeing in its face of luminous sky which of its windows were light or dark—or blue or purple.

She went on around the Circle and over toward the cut through the snowbank across from the marquee.

She changed into black slacks, a green blouse, black sweater, black flats. Wrestled the slim black flashlight out of its plastic-shelled card, fed the batteries into it, capped it, checked the on-off twist of its head. Bright light, neat design. Good New Thing.

She put it into her left-hand pocket, her card in the right.

She wouldn't need anything else. She'd only be up there a minute or two; they would either be there, getting ready for their blasphemous whatever-the-hell-they-did, or the floor would be dark. It wasn't as if she were planning to hang around and watch.

She had asked Al for the pill—he had given her two but she had only asked for one—just in case all the walking knocked her out. It hadn't; she felt wide awake, full of beans—adrenaline kicking in, probably.

Or maybe just the fact that it was only nine-fifteen. Which might be too early for more than one or two of them to be there, conceivably for some other reason.

She made a cup of instant coffee and turned on the TV—
to a news anchor touching his ear, listening. "We have word
now," he told her, "that there are fifty-seven known dead." He
sighed, shook his head. "To recap for you . . ."

Another Hamburg. Smaller. This time Quebec.

On Christmas Eve . . .

She sat sorrowing, shaking her head.

Half the channels had it coming in.

An anchor said, "No one has claimed responsibility."

"Asshole," she said.

She flipped past Jimmy Stewart dancing with Donna Reed
on the floor opening over the pool—sweet movie but twice
was enough—and watched some of *The God's Children's All-
Holy-Days Special*. When Andy started talking she flipped
away; didn't feel like watching him do his stuff tonight. She
thumbed back to news. The death toll was up to sixty-two.
She zapped it.

She stood looking out the window at the park's quilt of
snow—rounded shapes aglow with lights, laced with foot-
paths—wondering how Joe was faring out in Little Neck, at
Ronnie's table with Mary Elizabeth and her doctor. Would er-
ratic train service make him stay over? He hadn't volunteered
details about the marriage and its breakup, but she'd gathered
that the physical side hadn't been the problem. Would he be
spending the night in former-fashion-model Ronnie's room? The
thought stung—with surprising sharpness. A brake screamed
below; she heard the screams in St. Patrick's, banging, ringing.
She shuddered, hugged her arms.

Changed AMOURLESTS into LOSTMAUSER. Vaguely familiar.

At a quarter of eleven, she freshened her makeup and fixed
her hair—she'd had Ernie undo his inspiration, Andy had been
right—and took half of one of the pills, just to be safe.

She cracked the hall door and peered off at the concierge's desk; one of the women was on, she couldn't tell which, talking to a couple in coats. She drew the door closed and waited, looking at the framed hall map with its red emergency exits. She'd find hers somehow—ten feet dead ahead.

She cracked the door again and—as a few people came out of a door farther down on the opposite side—drew it closed. But cracked it, waited till the two men and a woman were near the desk, blocking her—and stepped out, closed the door with its DO NOT DISTURB sign hanging, crossed the hall, pushed open the glass-paned EMERGENCY EXIT door, went onto the landing, pushed the door closed.

The stairway was whitewashed cinder blocks and fluorescent lights. Holding a black metal banister, she climbed zigzag half flights to the eighth-floor landing.

Leaned her cheek to the door's glass pane.

She opened the door and went out into a softly lit hall— forest-green vinyl and sky-blue walls—like the hall on ten but half its width, and fully walled except for a large pair of doors across from the elevators and rest rooms.

She walked down there, to walnut double doors sealed with a giant brass GC logo. Saw herself askew, in black, in its polished surface.

She crouched, a hand to the floor; put an eye to the crack beneath the brass.

She stood, drawing breath, and took the flashlight and the card from her pockets. Reached the card to the slot by the door frame and ran it through; if it let her into Andy's private elevator it ought to open his front door for her.

Before she could touch the brass logo it split backward, the doors swinging open on darkness.

The flashlight and the spill from the hallway showed a large reception room—upscale furniture and magazines, doors all around.

She went into the room and turned, facing the elevators. Stood palming her forehead, trying to recall the ninth-floor layout from the day of the taping, over two weeks ago, and a meeting in one of the conference rooms a day or two after.

The conference rooms overlooked the park, which meant that the amphitheater was behind the elevators. Yes, they had gone out and back, around a curving wall; the rear of the stage ran parallel to the building's Broadway side. Which meant that the spiral stairs in the passageway between the dressing rooms and bathrooms—would be *there*—off somewhere beyond the northwest corner of the reception room, almost all the way back.

She followed her fluid disc of light through a door to the right, and down forest-green vinyl between walls of office doors numbered in the low 800's. At a fork, she went left; followed more forest-green vinyl past higher-numbered doors. Just about where she thought it would be, she found, in an alcove on her right, a black iron spiral to the floor above.

She mounted its wedge steps slowly, holding the handrail, pausing to listen—silence—keeping the light down, coming up into forest-green passageway, floor and walls carpeted. On the right, two doors a few yards apart, a pay phone on the curving wall between; on the left, two doors side by side, symboled bathroom doors, dark at the bottom. Light underlined the dressing-room doors; the nearer, the door to the women's, was open a crack, light from inside glazing its forest-green enamel. Coming out of the spiral, standing in the carpeted passageway, Rosemary sniffed.

Sniffed again.

Tannis, anybody?

She peeped into the dressing room.

No movement, no sound.

She opened the door farther. The booths, facing each other three and three, were open, curtains gathered at the sides. In the booth at her right, Diane's five hundred dead minks hung on a wall hanger alongside one of her velvet tents. Her jeweled watch and rings lay on a shelf, her black leather drawstring bag on the bench, black boots below. At the other end of the bench, black panty hose, tangled, stretched . . .

Craig's deep voice spoke in the green room; the door to it, beyond the empty chairs at the makeup tables, was only partway closed. He sounded as if he was asking questions. She leaned into the dressing room, a hand on the knob, a hand on the jamb, straining to hear. Couldn't make out what he was saying or an answer but caught a click from the hallway; stepped in, closing the door at her side as the men's dressing room door opened. She backed into Diane's booth, stood with her heart thumping.

Got a good breath.

In the booth opposite, a flouncy aqua suit, dead beavers, brown boots, a Gucci sack. Polly. Leopard-printed undies . . .

Silence now from the green room.

She waited.

Sniffed. The tannis tang seemed stronger, weaving through a jungle of perfumery—or maybe the pill, whatever it was, had sharpened her sense of smell. Colors too looked clearer.

Leaning around, she checked the booth alongside. Vanessa—electric-blue duffel coat, jeans, fuchsia sweater, brown hiking boots, black panties.

She leaned farther out; the booth next to Polly's was

Sandy's—dead coyotes, white leather boots, a pistachio dress. No undies.

She could leave right now. Did it make any difference whether Andy was there or not? They hadn't stripped to discuss GC's public-health programs for the year 2000—never mind at least two of the men being there. And the tannis smell was tannis, definitely, no mistaking it.

She took a good deep breath, to be sure.

Definitely tannis . . .

Silence still from the green room.

She stepped out and checked the last two booths; an empty beside Sandy's, another empty past Vanessa's—except for a long rust-colored robe hanging against the side wall she'd passed.

She stopped, stepped into the booth, studied the richly dyed robe. Raw silk, nubbly—supple between her fingertips. She drew a wide sleeve toward her; a cowl hung in back, a rust rope belt.

A monkish robe, lightweight, good lines, hems double stitched. She worked the label clear of the hanger's neck, squinted: MME. DELPHINE—THEATRICAL COSTUMIER.

She pinched a hair from the label, pulled it all the way free.

Held it up, seeing with her fresh, ultra-clear eyes the sleekness of the foot-long black filament . . .

She draped the hair over the shoulder of the robe.

She went between the chairs and the makeup tables with their bulbed mirrors to the partly closed door; moved behind it, and holding the knob, peeped through the hinge crack.

About fifteen feet away, almost directly in front of her, a little to the left, Sandy sat in the middle of a sofa, in a rust robe of her own, studying cards on an antique wardrobe trunk—tarot cards, for sure. She moved one, studied the pattern, sighed. Bad news from the beyond.

Tannis wafted through the crack; they were probably burning it as incense, in there or on the stage. Another rust robe passed close before her, left to right. "It's way past ten-thirty! I asked him specifically to start on time." Polly. "I *hate* staying up till the wee small hours; my internal clocks get all jangled."

Sandy gathered her cards, quick-shuffled, began laying them down again. Polly came back, sitting on the arm of the sofa, nibbling a cookie. She crossed bare legs out of her robe, good ones for her age, wiggled red toenails. Leaned her blond ringlets toward the trunk, bit her lip. Tsk-tsked.

Sandy sighed. "Always chaos, meaningless chaos . . ."

Enter third witch, left. "Has anyone seen Andy? He was here, now he's gone."

"It's way past ten-thirty," Polly said.

"I know," Diane said, coming to Sandy's other side. "The boys are getting antsy." Her robe was violet, dyed no doubt to match her eyes. She watched Sandy shift cards. Said, "What's 'lousetrasm'?"

"Nothing," Sandy said. "Chaos. It's a puzzle Judy gave me."

"Alice, you mean," Polly said.

"I *still* can't believe it," Sandy said, shifting her cards.

Diane, coming away from them, said, "Word games bore the shit out of me." She migrated rightward.

Rosemary drew from the crack, wide-eyed. Sandy hooked too? She turned. Andy held a finger to his lips: "Shhhh." She gaped; he covered her open mouth with his fingers. Whispered, "I was beginning to think you *weren't* putting me on." Grinned at her, gave her a kiss on the nose.

He took his fingers from her mouth, kept the hand raised for silence, winked at her as he opened the door tighter against her, easing out. "Ladies, would you mind? I need the room to myself for a few minutes."

"What for?" Diane, off right.

"Heavy meditation, okay? Out. Thank you all." A black robe for him, the same design as the others, from behind anyway, the cowl hanging down, the rope belt. The Sulka robe, downstairs in its giftwrap, would be sort of redundant; all the more reason not to give it to him, the cocky lying son of a—Satan.

"What were you doing in *there?*" Sandy asked, gathering her cards.

"Trying on boots. Polly . . ."

"You said we would start—"

"Start without me. I mean it, go ahead. *Yo, Kevin! Go sound!* Tell him."

He was closing the door to the stage when she went into the green room—ducking, glancing up at herself glancing down at her.

A theater or TV green room that's actually green is a rarity. One that's *all* green, forest green, in an all-forest-green theater—is a visual oxymoron. Or something. The low mirrored ceiling doubled the room's odd flavor. The offstage space had been decked; the control room for the light and audio systems was close overhead—along with everybody's upside-down reflection walking and sitting and schmoozing, or doing whatever they were doing in the forest-green green room.

Rosemary chose a chair by the sofa; sat straight in it, her elbows on its arms, her hands folded before her, fingers meshed, black-slacked legs together, black flats together on the carpeted floor.

Andy walked across the room—his reflection walking close

above him, pulling the black robes tight, cinching the rope belts—to the coffee and tea and the giant red Coke machine. "You want coffee?"

She stayed silent a moment. Said, "Black, please."

He poured coffee, poked the machine; a can clunked.

He brought her a GC mug of black coffee, with a spoon and a packet of sweetener; sat at the end of the sofa near her, popped the red can. Sipped from it.

She stirred the mug on the trunktop, eyeing Sandy's "cards," slips of three-by-five memo paper under a rounded silver paperweight. "You want the answer to it?"

She looked at him. "To Roast Mules?" she asked.

He nodded, smiling. "I got it in a week or so."

"*Don't you dare tell me!*" she said. "I'll find it myself!"

He chuckled. "Oh boy," he said, "do I have a hold over you. Watch out or I'll say it."

She put the spoon down, sat straight with the mug in both hands; drew a breath and sipped, looking ahead.

He put the can on the carpet, away from his bare foot; leaned closer to her. "I shouldn't tease," he said. "I know you're worried. Don't be. I only lied a *little*. I'm sorry. I was afraid I might scare you away again, after you'd been gone so long. Mom, look at me. Please."

She turned her head, looked at him.

He said, his eyes clear hazel, "What's going on here isn't Satanism. I don't worship him, believe me. To know him is to hate him; he lives up to his reputation. This is—trimmings, things I grew up with and like, that's all. Those were the only parties and holidays I knew. This isn't even witchcraft, we don't do spells or anything. It's no more Minnie and Roman's old-time religion than—than an office Christmas party is Rob Patterson's. Listen to that . . ." He nodded across the room.

Chanting had begun—coming from a speaker in the forest-green carpet between the tops of the dressing-room doors—an undulant chanting twined with odd, quivering overtones. "Do you recognize it?" he asked.

She cocked an ear toward the speaker.

"Did you ever—take part in any—"

She shook her head. "No," she said. "I heard though. Through the walls, and the closet. You know."

He nodded, smiled.

She said, "This is different . . ."

"It's one of the old chants," he said, "but Hank's done things with it electronically—that's his hobby, electronic music. That's exactly what I mean—taped chants, electronically enhanced." He smiled. "Play them backwards, you hear the Lord's Prayer."

She smiled, sipped from the mug. Glanced at him as he picked up the can and drank, his Adam's apple moving. She put the mug on the trunk, sat back with her hands on the chair arms, looked ahead. Crossed her legs. Sniffed. Fanned a hand before her face.

"It really *is* an office Christmas party," he said, setting the can back down. "Done the way Andy likes it. They accept it as an interesting, not so exceptional kink in someone who has to present a full-time public image of conventional goodness—a kink that Andy somehow *intuited* each of them could go along with, for his or her own reason. It connects in a way with those professional types coming down out of Dominique's Dungeon Monday night. At least according to Vanessa; she wrote her thesis on the subject."

He leaned closer to her. "These are talented people who do a world of good," he said, "and they ease the stress and let off steam with some unconventional behavior. They're no more

Satanists than you are; half of them are regular churchgoers. Jay's an officer of his synagogue." He put his hand on hers on the chair arm. "And they're not murderers, Mom," he said. *"And I didn't tell them to murder.* That's what you're most worried about, isn't it."

Looking at him, she nodded. "Yes," she said.

He sat back, shook his head, raked his tawny hair. "I don't understand," he said. "Why? I suppose you could say Judy *meant* to betray me last summer, but she didn't. We had absolutely no idea who she really was."

"She came to tell me something," she said, "not for a game of Scrabble."

He looked away, shook his head, sighed. Looked back at her. "Probably that she was ending our relationship," he said. "Things fell apart in Dublin. Guess which night." He picked up the can, drank.

"She'd already told me that," she said, watching him. "I think she was going to tell me about this."

"Mom, it's *nothing*," he said. "See for yourself, watch for a few minutes. Her robe is in there; put it on, pull the cowl all the way down, nobody'll know it's you. They'll think I brought someone, I used to before. You'll see, it's just a party with some druid chants and old dances and good eats. Black candles instead of red and green, tannis instead of holly— big deal."

She looked at him. Said, "Thanks but no thanks."

"Nobody would pressure you to do *anything*," he said.

"I said no," she said. "Even if it's as innocent as you—"

"I didn't say innocent," he said. Smiled. "I said not Satanism, and no pressure. Chances are William will grope you, but if you slap his hand he won't do it again. Muhammed's more persistent."

"And if Judy had gone to the media with just that?" she asked. "Just 'druidic office parties at GCNY'?"

He sat a moment, and got up and walked toward the dressing-room doors, draining the can under his upside-down reflection sucking at his.

He crumpled the can, tossed it into a wastebasket, turned and faced her. "It would have been an embarrassment, yes," he said. "but believe me, Mom, I never would have hurt her little finger to stop her. I really loved her—even after Thanksgiving."

She looked away. A drumbeat joined the chanting, slow and steady . . .

"And I don't believe she'd have done it," he said, going back to her. "She enjoyed everything as much as anyone. She gave us Yoga ideas we've made part of things." He crouched by her chair. "Come *on*," he said, his hand squeezing hers on the chair arm. "Just for a few minutes. For *us*, you and me. How can we go on having fun together, like today, with you thinking maybe I'm still lying and they're out there chopping heads off chickens?"

She sighed. "I wasn't thinking *that*."

"What were you thinking?" he asked.

She looked at him, blinked, shrugged. "I don't know," she said. "A 'Black Mass,' I guess. I don't really know . . ."

"What are you," he asked, smiling at her, "a cardinal who condemns movies he hasn't seen? Books he hasn't read?"

"Oh *God*, Andy," she said, "all *right*, you *win*."

She got up from the chair as he stood up straight, smiling, taking her by the shoulders with both hands. "I'm glad it worked out this way," he said. "It's like you showing me things in Ireland. These are *my* roots, sort of, some of them. I never thought I'd be able to let you see." He kissed her cheek; she kissed his, where his beard began.

"I'm only going to stay two minutes," she said. "It's been a long day and I'm very tired."

He watched her, smiling, straightening his robe, cinching his belt, as she went to the women's dressing room, her reflection walking upside down above her, in sync with the beating drum.

16

SHE STOOD hand in hand with him by the wall at the side of the stage, her eyes seeing farther into the dark, into the dusk of candle flames, pastel spotlights, dimmed red exit signs. A dozen feet away, cowled robes, sleeve to sleeve, sidestepped slowly back and forth, a circle wheeling counterclockwise. Voices trailed the airborne voices' undulant chanting, the drum leading, a fife or flute piping along, all entwined in reverberent echoes. Rust robes, brown robes, darkly the same in the forest shade, swaying, sidestepping—only the violet robe's wearer known for sure.

And the shortest robe's wearer, Jay.

And the tallest robe's, Kevin. Oops.

She glimpsed, beyond linked sleeves, the highlights of a dark chair. Whispered, leaning closer to Andy, "Is that Hank in the center?"

"No," he whispered, "I sit there. He's in the circle."

She turned her head, letting go his hand, drawing the cowl farther aside to look at him.

His bearded face wrapped in black, he nodded. "It's the only time he can stay on his feet more than a few minutes," he said. "I gave him a pep talk before." He smiled at her. "Stay till this is over, okay? Ten minutes, tops. They won't leave the circle." He kissed at her, and turned and went, his robe swirling about his bare heels, his Achilles' tendons.

She watched dark sleeves part and lift to let the black robe through; the sleeves slid down from pale arms, a wide silver bracelet glinting on the slim arm on the left. The robe's cowl turned her way—darkness, a shadow face—as the sleeved arms linked again. The cowl faced the other cowl; that one leaned its shadow face toward her as the circle of dancers wheeled farther counterclockwise.

Andy was sitting now, stage center, facing front, all black robe, glossed with pastel by the overhead spots—all black except the tip of his beard and his left hand on the chair arm. The violet robe lowered itself to a seat before him. Cowl facing cowl, they linked sleeves, while the chanters sidestepped to the beating drum. The cowls stayed facing, violet and black—then met, and parted. The violet robe rose, Andy's hand helping. He beckoned before him. A dark robe, brown, moved in from the circle; violet and brown changed places. The chanters sidestepped, the drum beat on.

Rosemary swayed with the drum, her sleeved arms away from her sides so the nubbly silk could brush her skin—incredibly sensitive all over. Maybe from the pill—or could it be the tannis? Or the combo; she hoped there was no danger there.

But she felt super, as fresh and loose as if she were in some disco with Guy, the bastard, back in the good times. Cowls turned shadow faces toward her; she smiled at them, knowing she was as faceless as they, if not more, beyond the spotlights' glow, the nearest candles yards to her side.

Had they guessed who she was? Or did they think Andy

had found a new girl already—perfectly understandable haste
in someone who had to project so much conventional goodness. She swayed more freely with the chant and the drum—a
foreign visitor he'd picked up in the lobby. Italian. No, Greek.
Melina Mercouri. Swaying, silk brushing her skin . . .

Pale fingers beckoned from two or three sleeves in the
circle. She shook her cowled head, smiling, swaying. Never
on Christmas . . .

The dance was simple—two steps forward and one step
back, with a variation on every fourth drumbeat. A slow-motion
folk dance, steady, unhurried. Hardly a challenge for Ginger
Rogers. She tried the step anyway, the carpet soft under the
soles of her feet.

What would Joe make of the scene? A case for the Vice
Squad? Maybe . . . but maybe not. She could also see him looking for a robe. He had an adventurous spirit that she really *liked*,
and lacked herself. The Alfa-Romeo, for instance.

Oh what the hell.

She snugged the robe, cinched the belt, fixed the cowl for
maximum coverage. Took a deep breath—and walked slowly,
slowly, along with the drumbeat, to the circle of robed dancers,
to parting sleeves, hands that took her hands warmly.

She danced with the circle, sharing its rhythm, finding its
steps, watching black-robed Andy and a rust-robed woman
holding hands, talking. She circled sidestepping past his shoulder, holding Vanessa's cocoa hand, greenish in the forest light,
its usually clear nails painted black or near-black. When their
arms swung, a chain bracelet rolled in and out under Vanessa's
rust sleeve—large round silver links.

The brown robe following Rosemary was tall—William or
Craig. She kept a firm grip on his hand, in case it was William the
Groper. Closing her eyes, she hummed with the chant, not caring

to parrot the syllables, dancing comfortably, answering some kind of mammalian herd instinct, all her senses awake . . . "Pssst!" Vanessa's hand squeezed hers and let go. "Andy wants you!"

He beckoned; she was almost in front of him, a brown robe rising.

She went with the drumbeat to a backless black seat; gathered the robe around her, sat on flat warmth.

Their robed knees touching, she gave him her hands, looked at him smiling at her in his black cowl. "I was hoping," he said.

"You knew damn well, you bastard," she said.

"My own mother? Shame . . ."

She said, "What do you say when *they* sit here?"

He looked at her, his smile fading. "I thank them," he said. "For everything they do for GC and for me. And I tell them how glad the rest of us are that they're part of the circle. And they say whatever they feel like—air a gripe or admit a mistake or just say 'Thanks, same here.' In the coven, they knelt before Roman, vowed undying loyalty to Satan and him, and he pricked his finger with a dagger and they drank a drop of his blood. You can see why it didn't grab me."

She sat silent, holding his hands, looking at him as he smiled again. "Here we kiss each other on the lips," he said. "Chastely. The ball's in your court."

She said, "Chastely is easy." Leaned, pecked his lips, was up, hands free, before he could help her.

The "good eats"—laid out by the rust robes after the dance, along the amphitheater's first high curving step—were only so-so: warmed-over standards from the kitchen downstairs and icky-looking pâtés. There was a terrific eggnog though, with a bit of a kick and a hint of tannis, served up at center stage out of a handsome silver punch bowl—not the hotel's plated stuff but the unmistakable real thing, simple, shining, sterling—stabbed with six or seven pastel light-beams on a table draped in forest green, where Andy had sat.

Violet-robed Diane did the serving, her cowl back from her feathered, lately darkened hair—looking great, flushed from the dance and obviously fully recovered from her bout with sciatica. She silver-ladled the creamy cream into everyone's silver cups as the robes all mingled and chatted, all the cowls back, Hank in his chair laughing red-faced at something William was saying, each with a silver cup in hand.

Sitting in near darkness on the top step, at the green-room side of the curve, Rosemary kept her cowl up, though there was probably no need to. No one had so much as glanced at her since Andy had shepherded her up there when the dance was ending. The two of them had eaten there, from plates he had gone down and gotten, along with cups of the terrific eggnog. They had both been ravenous, not having had much more than the pastrami sandwiches all day.

He came mountain-goating up the steps now with refills, a cup in each hand, all black against the light of the stage. She looked away anyway.

The robes had a tendency to slide open—which had become apparent when the dance sped up a bit after everyone had sat and talked with him.

He gave her a silver cup, sat on the step a few feet from her, closer to the curve's center, tucking his robe around him. "You can take the cowl off if you want," he said. "You're almost invisible, and anyway they know. Nobody thought I'd bring a date-date so soon, so who else could it be? Vanessa was sure." He sipped from his silver cup.

She lifted the cowl back, fixed her hair. "What's their reaction?" she asked.

"They're glad you're here," he said, "and they understand if you don't want to mingle. They hope you'll join in another dance but won't be hurt if you don't."

She sipped from the silver cup. "Meaning at another party or tonight?" she asked.

"Tonight," he said. "There'll be two or three more. Faster, different." He sipped from his silver cup.

"Oh," she said. Took another sip from hers.

"If you're tired, I've got some pills."

"No, no, I'm fine," she said.

"Harmless," he said. "I get them from Al downstairs."

"No, I'm fine," she said. "Second wind."

"Andy!" Sandy stood at the rim of the stage, peering up toward them. "Can I speak to you for a minute?" Sounding peeved.

He groaned, putting his cup down, getting up. "Back in a minute, I *hope*." He jogged down the steps, holding his robe around him.

Rosemary lifted herself, hitched at the silk, shifted, settled into a more comfortable position against the carpet at her back and beneath her, snugged the robe. She picked up the silver cup and sipped, watching Andy on the softly lit stage listening to some disagreement between Sandy and Diane. He strolled with them, his hands on their shoulders, to the far side of the stage, followed them through the door to the offices and storerooms.

She savored the creamy nog, sweet-tart and tannissy; savored the shimmery old-new music idling all around her, the druidic forest-primeval flavor of the candlelit stage—the spotlights dimming now as dark robes, Kevin and Craig, lifted the table with the punch bowl on it—*beautiful* silver bowl, Diane's or GC's?—and carried it into the corner beyond the green-room door. Clearing the stage for the next dance . . .

Faster, different . . .

Jimmy Durante had put it so well: *Did you ever have the feeling that you wanted to go and still have the feeling that you wanted to stay?*

She chuckled, recalling him.

High. *You are very high.* Slightly high, anyway. The rum or vodka or whatever was in the nog. Or maybe it *was* the tannis—in there and in the air. She hardly noticed the smell now, but braziers smoldered at the corners of the stage, their smoke swirling up into pastel pillars. Beautiful . . .

Like the time she'd smoked pot with Guy and it worked, that's how she felt—the music so ultra-clear, her skin so ultra-tingly, sensing the silk against it, the carpet *through* the silk—but in this instance with her mental faculties completely unfogged, sharp as a tack. She sipped from the silver cup. Could tannis and cannabis be related? A dark climber stopped two steps below. Bowed. "Please pardon me, Rosemary," Yuriko said. "I'm so happy to see you here. May I speak with you a moment while Andy's away?"

Sitting straight, putting the cup aside, she smiled and said, "Of course, Yuriko, please sit down!" She closed her robe more snugly. "I've been hoping we'd get another chance to talk."

"Thank you, so have I," he said, seating himself on the step below her, a few feet to her left, the angled planes of his cheek and jawbone gleaming in the light from the stage.

Extremely handsome. Forty-nine, divorced, two married children. She had checked with Judy the day after the impromptu party in Andy's office.

She'd seen *Hiroshima Mon Amour* not all that long ago, or so it seemed; the man in that had been an architect too. Yuriko was GCNY's, the amphitheater's designer; he oversaw the design of all of GC's worldwide projects and headed his own firm too, one of the most highly regarded in the profession.

"How go the computer lessons?" he asked, smiling up at her.

"They're one of my New Year's resolutions," she said. "Top of the list."

"I have only one," he said. "To slow down. I'm going to be fifty next year; that makes a man think. GC has no upcoming projects for me, I'm fortunate in having surrounded myself with capable associates—and so I've resolved to take some time off and 'smell the roses.' "

"I'm all for that," Rosemary said, smiling down at him, leaning forward, her hands folded on her knees.

"I watched part of the 'All-Holy-Days Special' tonight," Yuriko said, looking up at her. "Andy's part. I always do, even though I have everything on tape; it's somehow not the same, is it? I came away from it, as always, as from everything he does—I speak as if I'm unique"—he smiled—"I came away from it with a renewed sense that he truly is a celestial being, no matter how he tries to pretend he's a mere human. And of course, sitting with him tonight only strengthened the feeling. There's nothing I wouldn't do for him." He sighed. "I truly believe he's going to be ranked among the immortals," he said. "The Lighting, I believe, is going to be a watershed event in the history of humanity, and at the same time a magnificent work of art, all the greater because of its transitory nature."

"That's just how I feel, Yuriko," Rosemary said, leaning down closer to him. "I've told Andy that; I'm so glad you agree."

"Seeing *you* here tonight," he said to her, "makes me more certain than ever that he—and you too—are true divinities. I mean that with all my heart. What ordinary mortal could share this with his mother?" He gestured around them. "What ordinary mother could share it?" He smiled at her, dazzlingly. "Myths will grow around you. Does that make any sense?"

She smiled back her dazzlingest. "No," she said.

"I suppose the tannis is speaking," he said, still smiling.

"The tannis?" she said.

"The incense," he said, pointing. "It's derived from the leaves of an Egyptian plant that's a kin of the Indian hemp plant, the source of cannabis."

"I *thought* I was getting a little high," she said.

"Everyone is by now," he said, "but even when I'm not, I regard you as a celestial being—and so I sit below you. At your feet." His head of jet hair bent.

She gaped. Her toes kissed by surprise—a first, and not bad.

Yuriko stood, offered a hand to her, smiling. "Come dance again," he said. "This one is fun."

The robes were forming a circle in the candlelit, pastel-pillared dusk—violet and black robes coming onto the stage, Andy looking at her as she stood.

She watched her feet, holding the robe closed with an arm as Yuriko helped her down the steep steps. The music grew louder, a twining woodwind, a driving drumbeat faster than before.

When they reached the corner of the stage and stood face-to-face, he slightly taller, she said, "I'm sorely tempted, Yuriko, but I'm very, *very* tired, I've had an *incredibly* long day."

He bowed to her hand and kissed it, something touching the backs of her fingers. She said, as he stood straight, "What a handsome pendant."

"Isn't it?" he said, holding it forward from the V of his robe: a circle of silver, a teardrop bent on itself, hanging on a black cord.

She leaned to it in the forest shade. "Does it have a special significance?" she asked.

He said, "I don't know what the designer intended; to me it suggests life's continuity, the continuity of all things." He let the pendant fall against his chest.

"It's lovely," she said.

He smiled. "It caught my eye," he said. "I have another resolution now: to invite you to dinner in the new year."

She smiled and said, "I resolve to accept."

They smiled at each other as he withdrew toward the circle, bowing. She looked for Andy's black robe. No cowls for this dance, and a pale green rope or vine held in everyone's both hands.

No Andy, no black robe. Violet though, amid the dark ones. The drum jumped louder; the vine-linked circle stepped to its beat, began turning clockwise.

She watched a moment, then turned and went into the green room, winced against its light as she drew the door closed. The music shrank into the speaker on her right.

Andy sat looking at her, sitting on the sofa in his black robe, a cookie in his hand. "I thought you and Yuriko—"

She shook her head, blinking. Glanced above, headed across the room toward the snack table. "Why aren't you?"

He shrugged. "This dance can get raunchy," he said, "and Diane must have gone heavy on the rum. I was coming to get you, but then I saw you coming down with him, and I felt . . ." He shrugged. "I figured I'd wait," he said.

She took a handful of cookies, walked back toward the sofa. He moved over.

She sat down, put the cookies on the trunk in a heap between them. Sat back and nibbled one. "Do you know that tannis is related to cannabis?" she asked.

"You're kidding," he said. "I'm shocked. *Shocked.*"

She gave him a look. "No wonder you're hooked on all this

stuff," she said. "I never, never should have let you go over that first time, to Minnie and Roman's."

"I'm not hooked on anything," he said, turning to her, "and don't start blaming yourself; you had no choice." He watched her a moment as she drew a breath. "Plenty of women," he said, touching her shoulder, "would have just taken off as soon as they could, and left me with them, period."

She sighed. "Some, I guess," she said.

"Plenty," he said. Kissed her temple. She touched his hand on her shoulder; they smiled at each other.

He turned and picked up a Coke, drank.

She reached. He gave her the can; she put it to her lips, drank. Gave the can back to him. He put it to his lips, drank.

She sat looking at Sandy's rounded silver paperweight gleaming on the slips of paper. Shook her head as if to clear it.

"So are you satisfied now?" he asked, putting the can down, sitting back, his hand taking hers between them. "Did you find any Satanism out there? Any witchcraft? Did anybody pressure you to do anything horrendous?"

"No . . ." she said, sitting back. The drum drove faster, louder, from the speaker, through the door. "Is this Hank's too?" she asked.

"No," he said, "it's some French group, I think."

They sat back, listening.

He switched her hand into his other hand, put his arm around her shoulders. She settled back against him, sighing. Closed her eyes. He kissed her temple. Her cheek. The corner of her mouth.

"Andy . . ."

"One chaste kiss . . ."

Drum-driven high on a blissful tide, she opened her eyes to herself on the sofa, arms clutching his black-robed back, a hand in his hair as her throat was bitten. Closed her eyes . . . Held him tightly as he held her, skin against skin, his knees spreading her thighs. A jungle bird screamed; she looked toward the speaker and saw a sign. Froze seeing it.

She saw it straight through the mirrored ceiling—the only patch of blue-sky blue in all the forest green, a rectangle with black letters across its middle.

Below a crumpled red can.

Clinging to the inside of a basket of woven reeds hanging upside down between the bottoms of upside-down doors.

The sign's letters were reversed and it was a good twenty feet away but she read it in a flash—so distinctive it was, so much in the news and her mind lately—and in the same flash she saw what she hadn't been seeing all along through the tannis haze and the pastel spots: Yuriko's pendant, the bracelets, the punch bowl, the cup she had held and sipped from. The sign made everything crystal clear: TIFFANY & CO.

Andy's head lifted tiger-eyed, horns showing. "I thought you were ready," he said, the drum beating, the bird screaming.

She shook her head.

He slipped farther down, a leg to the floor; she pushed against his head. "No," she said. "Andy, I want to be alone, just for a few minutes. Please."

He rose up on a knee, looking at her, his eyes half-hazeling, the horns sinking in. "*Now*," he said.

"Please," she said.

He drew a breath. Got up from the sofa, closing his robe. "Whatever you say, Miss Garbo." He looped his belt, cinched it. Smiled hazel-eyed at her, his forehead smooth. "You're not going to run out on me, are you?"

"No," she said. "I just have to—adjust my thinking. A couple of minutes. Please."

He nodded, took a cookie, and went to the door to the stage; opened it—hands were clapping in sync with the drum—and went out, drawing the door closed.

She sat up, closing her robe, and put her feet to the carpet, shook her head, held it. Drew a breath, blew it out. Drew another breath. Shook her head.

Picked up the can, shook it, sipped.

Put it down and picked up the paperweight, hefted the mound of silver, checked its bottom. Put it down.

She got up and went to the wastebasket, closing the robe tighter, tying the belt.

Picked out the flyer caught in the basket's weave.

A triple fold of slick paper with the black TIFFANY & CO. across its sky-blue face. Inside—she held it farther from Blind Eyes—she was congratulated in italics on her purchase of a Tiffany cigarette lighter, informed that the repair department stood ever ready should service be required, and shown photographs of gold and silver cigarette and cigar cases in the same ribbed pattern.

William smoked cigarettes, Craig smoked cigars.

She went into the men's dressing room.

William had dressed casually: navy blazer with gold I ♥ ANDY button, gray flannels. The gold lighter stood on his shelf, a matching gold cigarette case in one of the blazer's inside pockets.

Another gold lighter lay on Craig's shelf, along with a silver cigar case. Out of stock on the gold. What a shame.

Multidialed gold Tiffany watches lay on two of the shelves, one with an instruction booklet beside it.

She went back out. The speaker was quaking with what

might have been the sound track of *King Kong*. She went into the women's dressing room, holding on to the flyer.

She hurried out of the robe and into her own things, trying not to tremble; put the flyer into her pocket and got out the flashlight.

On the way out she checked Diane's jewel-crusted gold watch. *Cartier*. You can't win 'em all.

She hurried down the black spiral, followed the disc of light down forest-green-vinyl hallway.

17

ON CHRISTMAS day in the morning, she called Joe and told him she'd been up all night and had a bitch of a headache; could they get together later in the day?

He was disappointed but sympathetic. He too had had a bad night. The train back had been stalled for hours; he hadn't gotten home till after three.

"Ahh," she said, "what a shame. How did it go?"

A sigh. "I don't know . . . She comes on very nice but I have the feeling she's a manipulator, regardless of her orientation, and I still think she's too old. Did everything go all right at Saint Pat's?"

She said, "Yes. I'll call later, okay?"

She called Andy. Got his message.

Called the Number, spoke to the chip.

Sipped coffee at the coffee table, scanning the *Times's* front page—the Quebec disaster, sixty-six dead, across the top half; below the fold, boxed side-by-side pieces about preparations for the Lighting parties at the White House and Gracie Mansion.

The phone rang; she picked up.

"Before you say anything—"

"No," she said, "before *you* say anything. Get down here. You've got ten minutes. And don't bother bringing Christmas presents." She hung up.

He made it in under nine. Buzz. But it had to be him, with the do-not-disturb on the knob. "*Come in!*" she commanded—standing before the Scrabble table and the window's chiffoned brightness with her arms folded, in the cobalt-blue velour caftan she had worn the night he came to her Waldorf suite—minus the I ♥ ANDY button. A workmanlike director had been her mentor at CBS-TV.

Andy looked at her and shook his head, blowing out breath, as he closed the door behind him. He came through the foyer— and spotted the Tiffany flyer and the della Robbia plaque on the coffee table, their blues almost matching, the plaque a shade darker. "Hey now," he said, going to them—Mr. Clean in new jeans and a snow-white GC sweatshirt, could you believe the gall? Fresh from the shower, hair still damp-dark, no time for the dryer.

"Don't you think you're overreacting a bit?" he asked, turning toward her, the whites of his hazels as white as his sweatshirt. Great willpower; like father, like son, no doubt. "Come *on*," he said. "I *mean*, you stopped us before the biggie, didn't you? And it was *us* not just *me*, let's not play games here—" He drew a breath, smiled at her. "Look, we both sniffed the tannis, we both drank the eggnog . . ." He turned his hands out, shrugged.

"From the Tiffany cups," she said.

He looked puzzled. Pretty convincingly.

She pointed at the flyer.

He went on playing dumb, glancing over at it, looking at her—just a puzzled Jesus wannabe.

"Andy," she said, "it's another boutique up there. The bowl, the cups, bracelets, watches, cigarette lighters . . ."

He held his forehead, closed his eyes. Whispered, "*Oh for shit's sake . . .*"

Persuasive. You could almost believe he hadn't known.

She went over to him and took those snow-white shoulders with both her hands—as tightly as she could, tight enough to make him show surprise that was definitely the real McCoy; he grasped her wrists, staring. She said, "Look me in the eye—with your real eyes, please—and tell me your coven or your gang or your inner circle didn't kill Judy."

They held each other, wrists and shoulders, his eyes tigering.

She looked into the black-slit pupils. "Go ahead," she said. " 'No, Mom, they didn't do it, it was five other people.' Go ahead. That's your line. Say it."

His tiger eyes stared, his lips pursed.

"Go on," she said, squeezing his shoulders still tighter, leaning up closer. "Say it and we'll do the biggie right this minute." She nodded toward the bedroom.

He pulled her hands from him—"*Yes, they did it!*"—turned, moved away. "But it wasn't my idea! I'm not a free agent!" He turned. "I have backers," he said. "You know that. Did you ever stop to think how much money they've poured into the Lighting? Forget the factories, the distribution, think about the commercials and specials and getting them seen by everybody. *Everybody!*" He came closer to her, his eyes still tiger. "We're talking about Bantu tribesmen on the Serengeti! Peasants in Outer Mongolia! Places where we had to put in roads to bring in generators to show them the first TV they ever saw! *Billions* of dollars! Billions!" He drew breath. "They didn't want to— see it put at risk."

"Andy," she said, "things have changed a lot, but since when do the angels run the show? *You're* the producer, *you're* the star, *you're*—"

He barked a laugh. "My angels aren't angels, Mom!" he said. Swallowed. "They're businesspeople, altruistic yes, but hard-headed when it comes to protecting an investment. Look, it's *done.*" He moved closer to her, his eyes still tiger; she folded her arms. "What can I do?" he asked. "I really was sick in the car, I wasn't faking that. And *nobody* told them to do it like *that*, that was Diane! She's batty; thirty-five years at the Theatre Guild and all the world's a stage! She twists Craig around her little finger, he barks and everybody obeys."

"But you're the one who told them to do it," she said. "You made them *able to do it*, the same way you made Hank able to walk."

He drew breath. Nodded. "Not the same," he said, "but similar. Yes. I'm the one who's responsible. Yes. I had no choice." He went to the coffee table, took a deep breath, and stood looking down at the flyer and the plaque. Shoved his hands into his pockets.

She stayed with folded arms, watching him. "I'm moving back to the Waldorf," she said.

He turned, his eyes still tiger. "Oh *Mom* . . ." he said.

"I'm not staying here," she said. "I'll borrow what I need from a bank till I get 'Fresh Eyes' up and running. I'm sure my credit rating is terrific."

"Then borrow and stay here," he said.

"No," she said. "I don't know what's going to happen once the investigation starts, I can't even *begin* to think about what

I'm going to say when they question me, but I want distance between us from here on in, Andy."

He drew a breath, blew it out, nodded. Lowered his head.

She said, "I don't want to put the Lighting in jeopardy either, though I'm not as insane on the subject as those non-angels of yours. I don't want us to have to deal with a lot of awkward questions this week, not when Ireland worked so well and all the numbers are so good."

He raised his head, looking at her, his eyes beginning to hazel.

"So I'll wait till next Saturday," she said. "January first. But I really don't want to see you, not till—things work themselves out somewhere down the line."

He stood looking at her with his hazel eyes; she turned to the table and the window.

He said, "Will we—light our candles together?"

She stayed silent a moment. "In the park?" she asked.

"No," he said. "If we're there, we're not at Madison Square Garden and the Abyssinian Baptist Church and everywhere else. And I don't want to do anything political . . . I think the best thing is to just stay upstairs, in my place. Joe too; I wouldn't expect you to come otherwise. We'll be able to see the whole show down in the Sheep Meadow, bird's-eye view, and I've got this great media room—you must have seen pictures—so we can watch everything on all the networks. It'll really be the best way to get an overview of the whole happening."

She turned. Took a breath. Said, "I'll let you know."

He nodded. Turned and headed for the foyer.

"Take the della Robbia," she said.

"Oh *Ma* . . ." He turned.

"Take it, Andy," she said. "They bought it, you didn't. And I really don't want it from either of you."

He went to the coffee table, swept the plaque with one hand into the other; swung it like a paperback at his side, walking to the foyer. Out and gone, pulling the door closed.

She let out breath, unfolded her arms.

She began to top off her coffee, had the spout of the not-real-silver coffeepot tilted nearly to the point of pouring—but took the clean cup from the tray and filled that instead, about three quarters full. Left the coffee black, unsweetened.

Began pacing back and forth between the foyer and the Scrabble table . . .

Slowly, holding the cup with both hands . . .

Frowning over it, sipping . . .

Funny, funny-peculiar, the way he had laughed when he said his angels weren't angels. They certainly weren't, those plutocrats who opted for murder in a noble cause. Hardly a new mind-set in human history.

Where had GC found enough hardheaded altruists to pour out *billions*? Were there thousands of million-dollar contributors? Hundreds who gave multimillions? She had never even tried to estimate the total production cost of the Lighting, never mind all of GC's other projects.

Andy had spoken as if the Lighting were the one and only, the be-all and end-all. Naturally he saw it that way now, under a week away . . .

She sipped, pacing . . .

Why hadn't she met any of those major backers? She'd

met people who gave thousands annually—at affairs in New York and Ireland, and at Mike Van Buren's on Thanksgiving day. Rob Patterson's Christian Consortium, she knew, was a significant contributor, but multimillions? She hadn't gotten that impression. A few million altogether maybe, over the past three years.

Wouldn't at least some of the top-level givers have wanted to meet her? Wouldn't Andy have wanted to oblige them?

Only that elderly Frenchman, René, at the airport, and maybe the man with him; their handshakes and few words had been the full extent of her contact with GC's non-angelic angels. René had certainly been giving Andy a devil of a time on the phone the morning she'd barged into his office; Andy had sounded well accustomed to placating, or trying to placate, the old man . . .

She stopped in the center of the room.

Stood for a moment. Swallowed.

Closed her eyes, put a hand to her forehead.

Drew a breath and opened her eyes. Turned to the coffee table. Moved to it, bent, put the trembling cup down, pulled the *Times* around to face her.

Stood looking down at the front page.

Turned, rubbing her forehead. Walked slowly to the Scrabble table. Church bells began bonging.

She stood wincing at snow-bright daylight shining through chiffon. Looked down at the tiles on the table.

Not the Ten.

The rest of the herd, the other ninety-two, lying mostly face-up from her hunt for the outcasts.

She fingertipped a tile, drew it out through others onto the table's margin of polished wood. Left it there—a B. As in bells bonging *Oh lit-tle town of Beth-le-hem* . . .

She fingered another tile, drew that one out too, giving the B an I alongside it. And an O . . .

Gimme a C . . .

Gimme an H . . .

Gimme an E, M, I . . .

She didn't see the other C. Didn't keep looking.

She went back to the coffee table, picked up the phone, tapped a number.

Said, "Hi, Joe."

She said, "A little better. Let's get together now, okay? Some-place we can talk but not here, I'm sick of this tower. I'll come there; I've seen pigsties, I won't faint."

She sighed. "Where's that Chinese restaurant? It'll be empty today."

She said, "I don't care about that. The food's good, isn't it? Where is it?"

"It's a dump," was what he had said. Off Ninth Avenue, a faded twelve-table restaurant with plate-glass windows and frozen ceiling fans, decor by Edward Hopper.

In a side booth, one of the two occupied tables, they toasted the holiday with Chinese beer and got the presents out of the way first. His was a huge, handsomely bound and jacketed book she had found in the hotel's Rizzoli shop—photographs and blueprints of classic Italian autos, including his Alfa-Romeo.

"Oh this is just *beautiful*!" he said, turning the heavy pages. "I didn't even know such a book existed! *Bello! Bellisimo!*" He leaned across the table and kissed her.

Her present was a small gold I ♥ ANDY pin with a ruby heart. Van Cleef & Arpels.

She sighed, said, "You shouldn't have . . ." Leaned across the table and kissed him. "I love it, thank you, Joe." She pinned it to her sweater while he and the waitress gathered the wrappings and he ordered for both of them, not using a menu.

"What's on your mind?" he asked when the waitress had gone.

"Something really heavy," she said, "and I don't want to worry Andy about it."

"A threat?"

"You could say." She looked him in the eye. "Judy dropped a few remarks," she said, "that make me think—now that I know who she was, and now that these things have happened in Hamburg and now Quebec—they make me think her gang might have somehow tampered with the candles. Or a gang in the Far East they had connections with."

He sat back. Blinked a few times, looked at her. "Tampered with the Lighting candles," he said.

She nodded. "These might be cases where someone lit one early, or maybe a store or a house burned with candles in it."

He sat looking at her. "The first two times ever," he said. "The candles have been around all over the world for months and these are the first two times one got lit or burned."

She said, "Maybe there's some kind of built-in timer. I don't know anything about biochemicals, I'm pretty sure that's what's involved here, but there are two parts to the candles, right, the blue and the yellow? Maybe they're more complicated than that. Maybe there's some chemical something that keeps them safe or unarmed or whatever till a certain time, and a few of the candles are a little off. And a few of those few were in Hamburg and Quebec . . ."

They looked at each other. Sipped from their glasses of beer.

He gave her a sidelong smile and said, "Do you think maybe

this could be a case of opening-night jitters? You're Andy's Mom, you want everything to go off picture perfect . . ."

"It might be," she said. "I hope so. But maybe it's more; we *have* to check it out, Joe. Do you know someone who could? Not in the Police Crime Lab or the FBI, though. Someone private, a forensic chemist who does consulting work. Someone like that. With access to up-to-date equipment."

"Did Judy really say anything?" he asked. "Or was this a vision?"

She looked away, stayed silent, looked back at him. "A little of each," she said.

They sat back as the waitress put plates on the table and doled out dumplings with a pair of chopsticks.

They ate, he with chopsticks, she with a fork.

"Aren't these good?" he said.

"Mmm," she said, eating.

"This is the worst time of the year to get *anything* done," he said, "let alone something as complicated as this; everybody's on vacation. The NYU School of Medicine is closed down, which is where the first person who comes to mind is on the faculty, a classic-car collector up in Armonk. If he can't do it himself, he'll know who can. Except he's probably in Aspen or someplace, he and his wife and kids all ski. Look, if you're this serious about it, then we should go to the FBI. I know guys in the office here, and they have the facilities in Arlington to do the job right and do it fast."

She shook her head. "I don't want to get Andy involved in a—whole investigation," she said. Covered her mouth with her hand, her eyes tearing.

"Hey, hey, aaah . . ." He reached across the table, patted her shoulder, her cheek. "Andy wouldn't be involved," he said, "not in any bad way. I'm sure he'd be the first one to—"

"*I don't want to go to the FBI*," she said. "Maybe I'm—hallucinating, you're right, and I don't want to open up a whole can of worms. Please, Joe!"

He sat back frowning, watching her as she pressed a paper napkin to her eyes. "Okay," he said. "I'll get after this guy this afternoon. He's in *something* with biochemistry in it, Dr. George Stamos. One of his lab assistants was making designer drugs, right there in the lab, until her boyfriend shot her. In '94. George has two Alfas but they don't come anywhere near mine."

He called her around five that afternoon. The Stamos family was away but their message said they'd be back Monday morning. "I didn't say why I was calling; he'll think I'm ready to sell the car, I'll be his first callback. You can't realistically expect to get any action before Monday anyway. But Rosie, the more I think about it . . . If Hamburg was a sample, then you're talking about something that could maybe wipe out the whole human race. *Nobody* is crazy enough to want to do that."

She drew a breath; said, "I hope you're right, Joe. Thanks for following through."

"No sweat. Feel better soon."

She went back to reading a trade paperback she had bought that afternoon in the Doubleday's on Fifth Avenue—*Biochemistry: The Two-Edged Sword*. She was up to the chapter on nerve gases and flesh-eating viruses.

The Stamos family was back from its skiing vacation by Monday morning—all except George, who was in a hospital in Zurich, in traction. Joe got his phone number from Helen

Stamos after he explained that it was about a favor for Rosemary, not cars, but he couldn't make the call till Tuesday morning because of the time difference.

That was the bad news he phoned to Rosemary on Tuesday afternoon. The good news was that George had immediately come up with the man for the job, a colleague who was a partner in a laboratory in Syosset, Long Island, that did free-lance forensic work in criminal cases. Joe had spoken to the man, telling him that he himself, as an employee of GC, had heard a candle-tampering rumor that he wanted to check out just for his own peace of mind; almost certainly nothing to it, but still . . . "He's going to check a few of them. He'll know whether or not they're clean by tomorrow morning."

She said, "You told him 'biochemicals'?"

"Yes. He says it's not impossible but would be an amazing feat for a gang of PA's to pull off."

She watched TV, thumbing through the multichannel mix—being told time and again by Andy and by herself, in ten-second and thirty-second formats, how moving and inspiring the Lighting was going to be, and how great it was that everybody in the whole human race was going to take part in the glorious, symbolic, artistic happening, and that the time to unwrap and light here in this area *is seven p.m. this coming Friday*, just do it along with the TV, any channel, don't miss the warm-up starting at six, and remember, out of reach of the kids. Andy winked at her. "Sick of these by now, right?" He chuckled, she didn't. "Okay, but it's *so* important," he said. "I ask you *please* to make sure that everyone you know lights at the right time; will you do that for me? Thanks. Love ya."

She wondered if there could be something he did, something

he projected, that she was immune to, because of their kinship. It seemed no less impossible than gases that could turn a person to jelly in fifteen minutes.

Joe had managed to get Wednesday-matinee house seats for the first solid hit of the Broadway season, a revival of a failed 1965 musical for which, ironically, Guy had auditioned back in the happy days before they'd moved into the Bram, when they were still living in his one-room walk-up on Third Avenue. The show was a charmer, as she'd thought then, but she had a hard time focusing on the first act; Joe hadn't heard yet from the lab in Syosset.

He went to phone his answering machine during the intermission. She smiled and signed a few autographs for people sitting nearby, then sat looking at her open Playbill.

Joe didn't get back till the house lights were down and the second-act overture had begun. "Clean," he whispered, sitting down in the seat alongside. She looked wide-eyed at him. He nodded. "Perfectly clean. No bio-chemicals. Not even any perfume."

"*Shhh!*"—from behind them.

She had a hard time focusing on the second act too, but clapped wildly at the end and joined with Joe in the standing ovation.

They hustled into a bar next door and found a foot-square table in a dusky corner. "He analyzed everything," he said, "the wax, the wicks, the glasses. Four candles—two from here, one from out of state, and one from out of the country. One hundred percent clean."

"You spoke to him?" she asked.

"The message was on the machine," he said. "Written report will follow."

"Whew!" she said. "That is one big relief."

"You know," he said, "I hate to mention it, but it's not con-
clusive. Don't forget there were fourteen factories turning them
out. There could have been tampering at one, or some, and
these were from another."

"No," she said, "my—impression was that *all* the candles
were affected."

"All? At all fourteen factories? You really thought that?"

She smiled, shrugged. "Opening-night jitters," she said.

The waiter brought them her Gibson, his Glenlivet.
"Cheers," they said, and clinked glasses and sipped.

"Thank you so much, Joe," she said. "I'm so grateful to
you." Kissed him.

"Where are we going to light ours?" he asked.

"At Andy's," she said. "I think. The three of us. Is that okay
with you?"

"Why wouldn't it be? Sure, there's no place better." He
smiled at her. "For lighting our *first* candles, I mean."

"Right," she said, smiling back at him.

"Should I pick you up at six and we'll go up together?"

"Just what I had in mind," she said.

"Happy New Year," he said. They pecked each other's lips.
He said, "Call me romantic, but I'm glad we wound up waiting. It's gonna be one great New Year's Eve."

What a load off her mind! Andy may have let GC's obsessed
backers push him into abetting Judy's murder—for
which there could never be any forgiving and forgetting, definitely not—but at least they were that, obsessed backers whose
goal was to do good, not his "old man" using him to win an
instant Armageddon.

She took a long, hot shower. Finally she'd get a good night's sleep. Weeks since her last one, with the trip and then Judy . . .

She ordered cocoa and petits fours from room service; sipped and nibbled amid satin pillows, watching preparations for the Lighting in a schoolroom in Argentina, at the Air Force Academy, the Wailing Wall, an oil rig in the North Sea.

The only thing bothering her, as she zapped the TV and snuggled into her warm satin cocoon, was a feeling that Andy was calling her—like the time his head got caught between slats of the crib and he called her without being able to call.

She snaked an arm out and lifted the handset of the phone— alive and humming; she put it back down. Snuggled into the satin.

Knew damn well it was herself calling him.

Should have taken a cold shower, not a hot one.

Mom! His voice, in pain, woke her. Daylight fringed the closed draperies.

She lay listening.

Felt him, less strongly, but certainly didn't *hear* him again.

She refused to let herself trick herself into calling him. Went up to the spa after breakfast and biked, jumped rope, swam—the glassy splashing in the window-walled pool masking all other sound.

The bothersome feeling faded away as she sat eating a club sandwich in the living room, watching the Lighting finally becoming real—and so much more richly than she had ever imagined.

All regular programming had been suspended. On every channel the Lighting music, the Lighting logo, the Lighting countdown in one corner or another: -30:44:27, seconds streaming, minutes melting. On every channel shrink-wrapped sky-blue-and-gold Lighting candles being ranked on tables and counters, sky-blue-and-gold Lighting banners being raised.

On the Princeton campus. In a women's prison in Hong Kong. In a casino in Connecticut, a hospital in Chad, aboard the *QE2*. In an Oslo department store, a nursery school in Salt Lake City.

Heads talked with other heads about the Lighting's beauty and significance, and about the discord and pain and sorrow that would be darkening the planet at this cosmic milestone were it not, thank God, for Andy, Son of Rosemary, shepherding us into the year 2000 as One Humanity, Refreshed and Renewed.

Reporters shoved microphones at people and asked leading questions—in a Bolivian shoe factory, a Hassidic community in upstate New York, a firehouse in Queensland, Australia. In St. Peter's Square, in a subway station in Beijing, in Disneyland, Mickey and Minnie waving shrink-wrapped candles.

Andy was probably watching upstairs. She sighed; they should have been watching together, regardless. Tomorrow night, watching the actual event with him, would be the peak experience of her life.

She surfed the channels, sipping a Coke, using the biochem book as a coaster. Mombasa, Iraq, Tibet, Yucatán . . .

Everybody in the world would be lighting clean, safe, GC candles!

The Amish *liked* TV, spoke readily into the mike about Andy, Rosemary, the Lighting, and the joy of tractors.

Even the dingbats waiting to be picked up by aliens in UFO's would be lighting their candles before leaving planet

Earth. There would be just enough time, a woman leading a California contingent of three hundred explained; Nostradamus had predicted they would be picked up in the *second* minute of the year 2000, not the first. Two goes with two, don't you see?

6+6+6

ON FRIDAY morning, calling him was reasonable; she had to finalize their arrangements, she'd never even given him a definite yes. And she wasn't imagining he was calling *her* anymore; she had enjoyed a good night's sleep at last. And good melon and coffee and croissant, there in the satin. Maria, who had brought in the tray, had been more excited than she. "I feel like I'm marrying *everybody* tonight!" she had said, laughing, opening the draperies on an overcast sky.

Rosemary tapped Andy's regular number and waited through his message, watching Lighting preparations backstage at the Metropolitan Opera House, -9:37:17. "Andy?" she said. "I want to discuss this evening." She waited, watching the scene at Yankee Stadium.

Beep, dial tone.

She tapped the Number, spoke to the chip.

Felt good having done it. She checked the crossword puzzle and felt even better; there she was—1 across, *Noted mother*, eight letters. The Lighting was the day's theme, naturally, and the rest of the puzzle—except 6 down, *Noted son,* four letters—was tough and tricky, the usual Friday challenge. Almost forty minutes before she finished.

He hadn't called.

She tapped the Number again, spoke to the chip, stayed on through the different-number option. "If you wish only to give a message to Andy, press two."

She pressed two.

"Please record your message for Andy now." *Beep.*

"Hi," she said. "I want to discuss this evening. Joe's picking me up at six; is that what you were figuring on? Call soon, will you? I have a hair appointment at eleven-thirty." She waited.

"Thank you, Rosemary. Andy will get your message soon. You may hang up now."

He hadn't called by the time she left.

When she got back to the made-up suite, there were double-digit messages on the regular line and one on the private line.

"Hi, do you know where that son of yours is?" Diane. "I haven't heard from him since Tuesday and the calls are pouring in. Some he's *got* to return—I mean, like the Pope and the President? I don't even know which site the two of you are going to; I assume the park with the rest of us. Would you please tell him to call me, or call me yourself if you know what's going on? And guess who's writing haiku about you. 'Bye."

She erased it.

Turned the TV on. Talking heads, at -4:14:51.

A plastic bag from the valet hung on the pull-out rod between the closet doors. She tore it open, drew free the sky-blue crepe, laid the pantsuit across the bed. She hung the other things away, and got out the gold silk blouse and the gold high-heeled sandals; put them on the bed too. Rolled the plastic up, popping it, and stuffed it into the wastebasket.

She stood frowning. Checked the pocket of her slacks for her card.

She put the shades and the kerchief back on.

Rode down to the lobby—jam-packed and noisy—and keeping her head down, made her way around the corner from the elevators to the AUTHORIZED PERSONNEL ONLY door; ran her card through the lock and pulled the door open.

She carded the elevator door; it split, the cab right there—suggesting Andy had gone out. Maybe he hadn't died of a heart attack after all while she ignored his calls for help.

She got into the inside-out lipstick anyway, turned, braced herself for lift-off, touched 52. Whoosh as 8-9-10 flicked past. She took the shades and kerchief off, fluffed her hair, waggled her jaw till her ears popped.

Remembered last time, facing his bearded chin, rocketing up with him faster than she liked—to the view et cetera.

The red 52 pinged alight as the cab slowed, and split open.

The sky beyond the black-and-brass lounge was wintry gray, darkening already at three o'clock, clouds growing heavier over distant Queens. More snow on the way?

"Andy?" she called as the brass cylinder closed behind her.

A woman spoke, a familiar, fluent voice, off to the left and back. " . . . with our continuous coverage of the Lighting. It's just under four hours away now, and everywhere, in every time zone, people are feeling a new solemnity . . ."

"Andy?" she called, following the voice back toward an open doorway. TV pictures shone and shifted in the side wall of the room within, four large screens she could see and parts of two nearer ones, three over three. *"Andy?"* she called, along with some kids in a classroom on the screen with the sound. She pushed the door all the way open, looking beyond it to the room's other side.

He was nailed to the wall. Nailed through his bloodied palms, his arms outstretched, his head hanging. In his white GC sweatshirt and jeans, standing sandwiched between the dark wood wall and the back of a black leather couch pushed against him.

She closed her eyes, swayed, holding the doorjamb.

Looked again in the shifting light at—not a vision—Andy crucified, small pale horns jutting from his bloodied hair. Dead?

She pushed from the jamb, rushed to the couch and on it on her knees, a hand to his chest, a hand to the side of his neck.

Warm.

And a pulse.

Slow.

Feeling the throb in the side of his neck, catching her breath, she winced at his right hand—the fingernails grown into claws, four inches of flat-headed metal thick as a pencil sticking out of the bloodied palm. What lunatic had done it? A track of dried blood trailed down the dark wood wall.

Were his ankles nailed too? She craned her head beside him but couldn't see into the dark behind the couch. His feet seemed to be on the floor, judging from his height and the moderate strain on his arms. She felt his chest stir. "Andy?" she said. Across the room behind her, he talked about the Lighting.

His head moved, turned toward her, the horns curving thumb-sized from his hairline. She caressed his cheek, wincing. His eyes opened. She smiled at him. "I'm here," she said. "I heard you. I thought it was my imagination! I'm so sorry, darling!" His mouth opened, gasping; his tiger eyes begged.

She turned to a low black console, put a foot to the floor, and lifted a dripping champagne bottle from a cooler, stood it aside. She took the cooler, turned with it and knelt on the couch again, dipped a hand into water, wet his lips.

She dipped water onto his tongue, into his mouth; he sucked water from her fingers, swallowed. "I'll get you down," she said, "I'll get you down . . ."

He sucked water from her fingers, swallowed, tiger eyes thanking her.

"Oh my angel," she said, "who *did* this to you? What beast could *do* this?"

His lower lip faltered against his upper teeth. "F-f-father . . ." he said.

She stared at him. Said, "Your—father?" She backhanded tears away, shook her head. "*He* was here? *He* did this to you?"

"*Is* here . . ." he said. "He *is* here . . ." His eyes closed, his horned head fell.

Maybe he was hallucinating, but who else could have committed such an atrocity? Vengeance for Andy's betrayal of his plan? For the candles being harmless?

Satan didn't jump out of the kitchen when she found it, or out of the freezer when she opened it.

She took out the whole plastic drawer of ice cubes, and went with them in search of the bathroom; found it by a bedroom with another window of wintry sky, both rooms ultramesso. In the bathroom she found a few fairly clean towels, a pair of barber scissors, and a bottle of rubbing alcohol; she snagged two neckties from an open bedroom closet.

Kneeling on the couch, she held a towelful of ice cubes close around his claw-nailed right hand and the thick iron nail sticking out of it. The nail had been rock solid before; there was no telling how far it went through the rosewood paneling and whatever was in back. She hoped the ice would contract the metal—and numb his hand against the worsening of pain that was already surely excruciating; wasn't that how it had earned the name?

She made herself wait, watching his sleeping, troubled-looking face. Had his horns sunk in a bit? Or was she getting used to them?

She shifted her chilled hands—the towel was wet through—making sure the ice stayed close against the nail and his palm. She shook her head, wondering at the cruelty of a being who could do this to *anyone*, let alone his own son. *He lives up to his reputation*, Andy had said. Surpassed it, rather; the worst she remembered from the Bible was "the father of lies." How about the father of bestial savagery?

She shivered, seeing again—first time in a long time—the yellow furnace eyes she had looked into for an instant that night while he pounded into her, the coven watching all around. Andy's tiger eyes, she had decided when he was still in his bassinet, were a golden mean between the extremes of those hellish eyes and her human ones; now it struck her that his less attractive traits and talents, like his lying and his power to sway people, might also be only half his father's. Nice thought.

She lowered the towel of melting ice, put it in the plastic drawer on the console, and got off the couch, wiping her hands on her slacks.

She dragged the end of the couch farther from the wall at his right side. No nails in his ankles. She felt to be sure—socks and sneaker tops, no nails.

She stood with her back against his hip, her shoulder under his arm; wrapped a band of dry towel around the inches of nail sticking out of his hand, and grasped the wrapped, cold metal with one hand over the other. "Out," she told it, and pushed at it and pulled at it—slowly, not too hard. Andy moaned as the blood track below his hand freshened. "Got to do it," she said. The nail moved; she pushed and pulled with one hand, bringing his hand along with her other, and as gently and carefully as she could, began dragging and twisting the nail out through his skewered hand, holding it still against the wall. Seven, eight, nine inches long the damned thing was; she tossed it away; it clunked on the carpet.

She wrapped another piece of towel around his hand, tied it with a necktie, tight, and turned toward him, pulling his arm over her shoulder, trying to figure out a way to keep him steady while she got over the back of the couch to his other hand; but his arm raised and reached over her. She ducked, watching him, supporting him against the wall, as he turned and reached to the nail sticking out of his other palm. She said, "Ice first," but he clutched the nail with his towel-wrapped hand and pulled, his eyes squeezed shut.

She turned away, wincing—wood and masonry squealed—and she caught him, almost fell under him but got him up and draped over the back of the couch as the nail banged off the console. She bent, hugged his jeaned legs and hoisted them, hefted him up and over, darting around the end of the couch, stopping him, bracing him facing the back of it.

She lowered him onto his back—out cold—and tugged him farther down the couch so his ankles were on the padded arm and his head low against the other arm. She wrapped his bleeding left hand in a piece of towel, tied it and put it at his side, fixed his other arm. Stood watching his GC sweatshirt rise and fall.

Took a good, deep breath herself, pushing her hair back.

She untied his sneakers and took them off, rubbed his socked feet.

Checked the Lighting countdown as she left the room: -3:16:04.

She got soap from the bathroom and a bowl of warm water from the kitchen and went back to him; unwrapped one hand and then the other, picked the conspicuous bits of stuff out of both sides of his wounds, washed them, trickled alcohol on them; wrapped them tightly with fresh lengths of towel and retied them.

She unfolded a faded crocheted afghan over him, remembering it, she was pretty sure, from the Castevets' living room.

He needed a tetanus shot, surgery, hospital care; how could she get it for him with his horns and claws and eyes showing?

She would have to trust Joe with the truth, there was no other way. Maybe, just maybe, he knew a doctor who could be trusted, or bribed eventually to stay silent, or of a private clinic somewhere.

She washed Andy's face, and the blood from his hair; separated the hair and dabbed at a swollen inch-long line of dried blood; left it as it was.

She brought things back into the kitchen, washed her hands

at the sink, and blood from her sweater; put the drawer back under the icemaker and flipped it on, filled a glass with cold water. Drank some, refilled it.

She put the glass on the console and sat down on the floor by the end of the couch. Felt Andy's forehead. Cool, but not too. She touched the tip of one of his horns—ivory-ish, sort of.

She leaned back against the end of the couch, rested her head against the arm, close to his head lying against it. Sighed, closed her eyes. Listened to a muezzin's call to prayer segue into cantorial singing, an operatic tenor.

She opened her eyes and watched four different scenes on six screens—twin temples, a stadium with Egyptian signboards, the grand stairway of the *QE2*, twin shots of the crowded Sheep Meadow downstairs—all the counters down to -1:32:54 and running. Red digits on the console gave a translation: 5:29.

She hadn't realized it was so late, but cutting the towels, cleaning the wounds . . . Joe would be on his way by now, or almost; no point in calling him. He'd surely assume she had gone up early and would come right up himself.

She watched the screens, listened to the talking heads, the anchors, the Mormon Tabernacle Choir.

Andy's head turned; she turned hers; his tiger eyes were watching the screens. "Hi," she said. "Nice to have you with us." He stayed silent, watching. "Thirsty?" she asked.

He made a sound in his throat.

She knelt, cradling the back of his head, holding the glass while he drank. "Joe's going to be here soon," she said. "There's a good chance he'll know someplace where we can get you some medical treatment. You're going to be fine."

She lowered his head, put the glass down.

He watched the screens.

She said, "It's going beautifully"—shifting around and leaning back against the leather couch arm again.

Their heads close together, they watched, listened. "Ah, look . . ." she said, smiling. He cleared his throat. "Three minutes after they're lit," he said, "the candles begin releasing a virus that's suspended in a gas. It spreads . . ."

She turned to him. "A lab said they're clean . . ."

"Then they didn't know what they were looking for," he said. "That's why I was nailed there, to keep me from telling you while there was still time to get the word out. I was going to." He swallowed, looked at her. "I feel so rotten about it," he said. "I keep thinking about that kid James . . ."

She stared at him—as the Lighting music swelled, the choir singing out.

"Rosie? You here?"

"Joe!" she called. "Wait a second!" She started to get up; Andy's bandaged hand caught her arm. "I feel so *guilty*, Mom," he said, his tiger eyes tearing. "Lying to you, keeping everything from you—about the candles, about him—I just wish I were dead!"

She turned from him to Joe coming in the door, tall and dapper—ultra-dapper—in top hat, white tie, and tails, a bundle of sky-blue-gold silk in one white-gloved hand, a picnic hamper in the other. "Funny," he said, dropping the bundle on a chair, "I always thought this would be a festive occasion, but now, when it's finally here, I all of a sudden feel—I guess 'grave' is the word for it. Hmm." He planted the wicker hamper on the console. Took off his top hat, put it crown down alongside. "You," he said, pointing a white-gloved finger at Andy, "are lucky you have such a loving mother, because if it was up to me, you'd spend the rest of eternity nailed to that wall."

Rosemary, on her knees, holding onto the edge of the console, looked up at him. "Joe?" she said.

"Hi, puss," he said, smiling down at her, tugging at white fingertips. "Tonight's the night." He winked a yellow furnace eye at her.

Smiled at her as she climbed to her feet staring at him, while Andy muttered.

He dropped glove one into the top hat, tugged at the fingertips of glove two. "*Had* to come along with him," he said, smiling at her. "Couldn't trust him to run the show himself, could I, him being half human, liable to go soft? Not with so much at stake, no way. And was I right or was I wrong, I ask you?" He dropped glove two in the hat.

She stared at him.

"I knew the dentist would get a cab or something thrown at him," he said, straightening his white tie. "I know the way that mind up there works. This is mega-chess, the endless game; he's white, I'm black. He got first move but tonight I wipe out his pawns." He smiled at her. "His knights and bishops too, and the king. The queen I keep." He bowed to her, winked. "That worked out neat, didn't it? You were his logical move to make mush out of young Eat-a-pussy here, so I had Joe Maffia ready and waiting for my countermove."

She stared at him.

"Who's a lady in distress likely to turn to," he asked, duding up his shirt front, "if not an ex-cop with just-maybe mob connections? Could anybody be more useful if she needs, say, a forensic chemist? Or house seats for a hit or a Mass? Oh hey, regards from Mary Elizabeth and her lesbian lover!" He grinned at her. "When *I* step into a cathedral, baby," he said, "*everybody* has a seizure. But enough about my devilish machinations. Pride! I just can't seem to shake it." He shook his head, picked up the sky-blue-gold bundle, unfurled her pantsuit and blouse, drew out the sandals; offered her both handfuls.

She looked at them, at him.

"Go change," he said. "And fix yourself up; he's got the complete works of Elizabeth Arden in the guest bathroom. Over by the elevator."

She stood staring at him.

"Come on," he said, smiling. "Lighten up, like he says in the commercials. We'll dance a little. It's a better warm-up than this bullshit. That's a great floor out there; it's where I taught him. Ballroom is one of the few things you guys do that's nice to look at."

She drew a breath. Said, "I would sooner die. Honestly. I mean it."

"Oh?" He lowered both handfuls, nodded. "I can see how you would feel that way," he said. "It's your species, after all. Plus the Catholic upbringing." He nodded, looked at one of the nails on the carpet. Squinted at it.

The blood-streaked iron nail rose in the air, drifted aside, rose higher, and hung with its head against the ceiling, some nine or ten feet above Andy's face. He lay looking up at it.

"Which eye?" Joe/Satan asked, looking at Rosemary, not at the nail up above.

She put out her hands.

"**J**ust relax. Remember? I do all the work."

They danced on the slick black floor before the glittering diorama—the East Side, the Whitestone Bridge, Queens, the whole shootin' match—under the luminous bottoms of rolling clouds.

He sang along with Fred Astaire: "*Before the fiddlers have fled, before they ask us to pay the bill, and while we still have the chance . . .*" Held her closer, her waist, her hand. "Hey listen," he said, "I'm sorry I was so obnoxious in there. It's a very special night for me, you've got to understand that, and I'm kind of keyed up. And I'm not accustomed to getting backtalk, except too much of it lately from him."

"So you nail him to a wall," she said, not looking at him.

They danced, a piano and orchestra leading them.

"Look," he said, "I could have had the coven do the sensible thing with you way back when, but I didn't; I made it the coma, and made sure you were in a good place and the bills were paid." He turned her as she looked away. "We looked into each other's eyes that night," he said, "and don't tell me you don't remember. It may have been a scary moment for you, an awful one, I'll grant you—but it was an exciting and beautiful moment for me. Once in a lifetime—one of mine, not yours, if you follow me—which you're doing better now, see? And who knows?" He dipped her, lifted her. "Maybe I'm even smarter than I think I am. Maybe I knew, or just hoped somewhere deep inside, that if you were alive when the time came for Andy to begin his work, it might turn out that we'd look into each other's eyes again, in a nicer, more civilized situation—that there was the possibility, so to speak, of a sequel for us."

She looked at him; he smiled at her. "See, we're looking," he said, turning her. "You like *his* eyes? I can do tiger." He tiger-eyed her. "You like Clark Gable?" Clark Gable asked her, dimpling at her, turning her. "I can play Rhett Butler all night long, Scarlett." Gable grinned his roguish grin, dipping her. "Up the stairs and never a fadeout." Joe/Satan lifted her. "My effects," he said, "are very special." He winked.

She looked away; he twirled her out and drew her back. Astaire sang, "*There may be teardrops to shed . . .*"

"Now we're getting to the good part," he said. "In case you haven't seen where this is heading . . . I'm talking about Eternal Youth, Rosie. Pick your age, twenty-three, twenty-four, whatever you like, and it's yours forever. No aches, no pains, none of those pesky little brown spots, everything ticking along like the motor of a Rolls." She looked at him as they danced; he nodded. "What I always promise and rarely deliver," he said. "You're old enough to appreciate it, aren't you, and I'll deliver it for you—not only the years you lost but the years ahead, all of them, in a lovely environment totally different from the hellfire crap you've been handed all your life. Room service that leaves this place at the starting gate."

Turning with him, she said, "Would you stop the Lighting if I—"

"Oh please," he said, "don't start *that* business. No I wouldn't. And I can't, it's too late. So it's Eternal Youth, or death when you go downstairs. The gas spreads and stays around; it's heavier than air; that's why we're up on top here."

She drew back in his arm, looked at him. Said, "What about Andy?"

He shook his head. "He stays," he said. "I don't need him anymore and I can't trust him, especially where you're concerned. We can have other kids, all you want; young forever, remember? Think about it, Rosemary. I know it's a tough decision for you to make, given all the circumstances and your background and everything, but you're an intelligent person who can put things together—you knocked me for a loop when you worked out that stuff about Judy—so I'm sure you'll see it's the only decision that makes sense."

They danced before the glitter and the clouds. He turned her, held her, put his cheek to hers. "*Heaven, I'm in heaven, and my heart beats so that I can hardly speak . . .*"

In the shifting light of the screens, Rosemary sat bent in a chair, her hands folded, her head down.

Andy reclined on the couch with an elbow on the arm and the afghan thrown back, watching with tiger eyes—shaking his horned head, lowering his lips to the straw sticking up out of the Coke can squeezed between the clawed thumb and first finger of his towel-tied hand.

Joe/Satan leaned back in a chair with his feet in black silk socks on the console, watching with furnace-banked-down-to-tiger eyes, eating caviar out of a pound tin with a spoon. He checked his multidialed watch, taking care not to tip the tin. Swallowed and said, "Son of a gun, three minutes and twelve seconds and there they go. Look, the guy on the steps. See? And there, over there, that woman. Uh-oh, look where the candle landed." He shook his head, stuck the spoon straight up in the caviar. "Incredible, the way they can time something like that." He picked up his glass of champagne. Sipped. "Those guys were really good," he said. "Where you going?"

Rosemary left the room.

She walked all the way through to the window.

Stood there, her forehead against the glass.

Gold dust lay sprinkled over the park fifty-two floors below, gold dust on the ball fields, gold dust in the Sheep Meadow, gold dust glittering as far north as she could see, thinner in some places, puddled with black in others.

Half the city—GC's inner circle among them—must have gathered to light their candles down there under the leafless midwinter trees. Drawn by druidic memories?

Fire burned in two windows in the Fifth Avenue cliff. In Queens, a red glow tinted the clouds.

High above, slow-moving lights crossed a cloud gap of starry sky—one of the few international flights that couldn't be rescheduled to avoid the hour. But the pilot would have gone back and lit one token candle for all the passengers and crew members, who planned to light their own candles when the plane came down.

Far below, a tiny horse toppled over on the gold-dusted park side of Central Park South, pulling its carriage over with it. Other horses and carriages lay in a row behind it. Cars and busses stood still, dark flecks and gold dust beside them.

She wept.

If she had come up here Wednesday night, when she had first heard Andy calling . . . If she had not had her guilt to confuse her . . .

She shuddered.

Drew a breath. Wiped her cheeks with the heels of her hands. Stood tall and looked out, counted six windows with fires in the Fifth Avenue cliff. Flames now in Queens.

She heard him behind her. *Get thee behind me, Satan.* She said, "I'm staying with Andy."

"And here I thought you were smart," Andy said.

She turned to him.

They looked at each other.

"Go," he said.

"How *can* I?" she asked him. "I don't even deserve eternal old age. I don't even deserve a day more of *now.*"

"Go," he said. "Believe me, it's what you should do. You'll be okay."

"Okay?" she said, her eyes tearing. "I'm going to be *okay?* With *everybody in the world dead*, and *you* dead, and me with *him?* You're crazy from hunger! You're insane!"

"Look at me," he said.

She looked at him. Into his tiger eyes. He said, "Trust me on this one."

She peered at him. Said, "Really?"

He smiled. "Would I lie?"

They smiled at each other.

She leaned to him, caressed his cheek. She tiptoed, he bent; they kissed lips, chastely.

Smiled at each other.

He stepped aside, raising a wrapped hand toward Joe/Satan, waiting by the open brass cylinder in his white tie and tails, holding his top hat.

She stood a moment and walked—crepe swaying, high heels clicking—across the slick black floor to him.

He ushered her into the red-and-brass cab. She turned— glimpsing Andy standing before the glitter and the clouds, a hand raised—as Joe/Satan got in close against her and the cab closed behind him.

They dropped.

He put his top hat on her head, tipped it back, fluffed some hair out from under. "Cute," he said, smiling down at her.

She looked ahead at his white tie. Really tied, no clip-on. "How do we get through the gas?" she asked.

"Not to worry."

She looked up at him smiling at her, red 10-9-8 flicking above his head, L-B-G1-G2 . . .

The cab dropped faster.

Grew hotter.

Starting to sweat, she stared ahead at his tie.

"I can't wait to get out of this monkey suit," he said. "The one *inside*, I mean. Three damn years now I been wearing it." His hands clawed—clawed—at the tie and the shirt collar, ripped them apart, tore them away with parts of his neck from green-black scales; flung fabric and flesh on brass and red leather.

She stared up into furnace eyes, white horns arcing. "You said it wasn't hellfire!"

"Rosemary, baby," he croaked, tearing jacket, shirt, flesh from wet green-black scales, "*I LIE! Don't you know that by now?*" He waggled a giant tongue in her face; she shut her eyes and screamed, his arms hugging her. "Ro! Ro!" he cried, holding her, hugging her, kissing her head. "You're okay! You're okay!"

She opened her eyes, gasping, panting. "You're okay," he said, hugging her, "you're okay, you're okay . . ." She clutched at her paisley pajama top, at a hank of her auburn hair, looked around, gasping, at the room in its early-morning light.

At the posters of Paris and Verona, the yellowing full-page ad for *Luther* with the red circle near the bottom.

She collapsed against his chest, gasping, sobbing, catching her breath. "Oh Guy!" she said. "It was *awful!* It went on and on, and I slept, and it started again, and went on and on . . ."

"Ah my poor baby," he said, hugging her, kissing her head.

"It was so real!"

"That's what you get for reading *Dracula* in bed . . ."

She leaned from his arms and looked down at the paperback

on the floor. "Bram *Stoker!*" she cried. "Of course!" She caught her breath as he sat back beside her. "We got an apartment in this old house called the *Bram*," she said, "the Bramford! First it was midtown, then it was on Central Park West, first it was black, then it was pink, it had gargoyles, it *didn't* have gargoyles—basically it was the Dakota, only it was rent-controlled."

"Wouldn't that be loverly," he said, lying back on the bed, yawning, scratching under the waistband of his paisley pajama bottoms.

She turned around and punched at his shoulder. "And you, you rat fink," she said, "you lent me to a bunch of witches!"

"Never, never!" he said, catching her fist, laughing.

"And I had a baby by Satan!" she said.

"Uh-oh," he said, pushing her down, climbing over her, "if this is turning into the baby conversation, I'm busy."

He got off the bed and stepped into the bathroom, pulling the door half closed as she hitched on her knees to the gilt-framed mirror canted from the wall at the foot of the bed. "Oh *God!*" she said, clapping her chest, leaning close to the glass. She stroked her cheeks, grasped her hair, kissed it, eyed her eyes, fingered the skin around them, caressed her cheeks, her throat, her hands. "I was *fifty-eight!*" she said. "I didn't *look* it but that's what I was supposed to be! It was *awful!* I looked like my Aunt Peg!"

"Isn't she the cute one?"

"Yeah, but still—fifty-eight?" She whistled. "Wow, what a relief to be young again! It was so real! The whole thing!" She sat back on her haunches, frowned. "It was 1999," she said. "It was weird. My son and I, we were like . . . like Jesus and Mary . . . but *very* different . . ." She shook her head, kneeled and studied her cheeks again. Looked really close at them.

Checked a teensy spot. "I've got to take better care of my skin," she said.

"It's good I'm up early. I'm going to go to that open call for *Drat! The Cat!*"

"It was a hit in 1999," she said, checking around her left eye. "A revival."

"I'll tell them, they'll be thrilled. I mean it, it's a great line to come on with. 'Gentlemen, I'm happy to announce you've got a hit! My wife is a psychic and she dreamed last night that there's going to be a revival in 1999!'"

"Since when am I a psychic?" she asked, looking in the mirror, folding her side hair up and under.

"Hey, this is show biz, remember?"

She said, "The skates had all four wheels in a line."

"I won't tell them that."

She chuckled. "There was a big gold tower at Columbus Circle," she said, looking at the other side of her head with the hair held shorter. "That's where I lived in the part where I was old."

"Where was *I* then?"

"Either dead or not famous," she said.

"Same thing."

She smiled at his little joke. Said, "I just may let Ernie cut my hair . . ." The phone rang; she turned, flopped down, found it on the floor on the second ring, picked up the black handset. "Hello?" she said.

"Hul-lo, my angel! Sorry if I woke you."

"Hutch!" she cried, rolling over on her back, stretching the cord. "You can't *imagine* how glad I am to hear you! I had the most awful dream, a coven of witches cast a *spell* on you!"

"It was prophetic, that's exactly how I feel; I was out on a bender last night and I'm at the Racquet Club trying to steam away the aftereffects. Gerald Reynolds is here. Tell me, have you and Guy found new digs yet?"

"No," she said, sitting up, "and we're desperate. We have to be out by the end of the month; that's when everything gets shut off."

"You shall bless me, my child. Do you remember my telling you about Gerald's apartment? With the jungle and the parrots? In the Dakota?"

"We were just *talking* about it!" she said. "The Dakota, I mean! Not—the apartment . . ." She clasped a hank of hair, held the handset, looked ahead.

"He needs someone to sit it for at least a year, maybe more. He's going home to work on a film with David Lean. He's absolutely desperate for someone responsible to tend the flora and fauna. He's supposed to leave the day after tomorrow; he had a cousin ready to move in but she was hit by a taxi yesterday and will be in hospital for at least six months."

Guy leaned around the bathroom door, half his face bearded with lather. He mouthed, "*An apartment?*"

She nodded.

"Are you there?"

"Yes," she said—switching hands on the phone as Guy sat beside her; he leaned to listen with her, holding his razor. "It's *rent free*, my angel! Four rooms in the Dakota, overlooking the park! You'll be in among the celebrities: Leonard Bernstein! Lauren Bacall! One of the Beatles is dickering for the apartment right next door!"

They looked at each other.

She looked ahead, grasping hair with her free hand.

"Do you want to discuss it with Guy? Though what there is to discuss, I can't imagine. Seize the moment; there's another chap here waiting to call someone about it. I'll hold, I have a nickel, but I'm getting glared at. Oh, before I forget, Roast Mules? Exactly three minutes and twelve seconds by the clock."

She lowered the handset a few inches.

They looked at each other.

"Ro," he said, "you can't possibly be thinking of letting a *dream* stand in the way. Nobody would! Rent free? The Dakota?"

She looked ahead.

ACKNOWLEDGMENTS

I'm grateful to Alan Ladd Jr. and Andrew Wald for getting me off the couch and over to the computer, and to the following people for advice, patience, and friendship, at least two out of three in each instance: Adam and Tara Levin-Delson, Jed and Suzanne Levin, Nicholas Levin, Phyllis Westberg, Michaela Hamilton, Howard Rosenstone, Wendy Schmalz, Patricia Powell, Herbert E. Kaplan, Peter L. Felcher, Julius Medwin, and Ellie and Joe Busman.

Roast Mules was laid upon me at a wedding seven years ago by a man I know only as the father of the actress Bebe Neuwirth. I cursed him for a long time—mildly, because of that daughter—but now I'm grateful to him too. The solution to the puzzle is honest and pleasing. Save your postage.

I.L.

New York
1997

AFTERWORD
BY NICHOLAS LEVIN

THIS PIECE CONTAINS MATERIAL SPOIL-
ERS FOR BOTH *ROSEMARY'S BABY* AND *SON
OF ROSEMARY*—PLEASE READ IT ONLY IF
YOU'VE ALREADY READ THEM, AND/OR
ARE OKAY SEEING THEIR PLOTS FREELY
DISCUSSED.

Critics (and let's be honest—many readers) greeted *Son of Rosemary's* ending with something less than rank enthusiasm; quite
the opposite. If its events were all just a *dream*, the thinking
went, that meant that *Rosemary's Baby* itself had *also* been just a
dream. And that meant that none of it was *real*. None of it had
happened. Ira Levin had committed *infanticide!*

This despite the fact that the central act of *Rosemary's Baby*—
Rosemary's rape by Satan—is ultimately revealed to have been a
dream *that was not a dream*. As Rosemary so aptly put it: *"This
is no dream [. . .] This is real, this is happening."*

Would Levin (my father) really have abandoned his *fic-
tional* child down in the *Bramford's* basement? Hurled him out
the seventh-floor window, as Rosemary contemplates? Was this
particular *'Son'* an *Abraham*-like sacrifice? Or, was Levin in fact
floating little *Moses Woodhouse's* black bassinet down the Nile
for safe keeping?

The author Chuck Palahniuk has mused over what he's found to be a beguiling sense of *predetermination* present throughout *Rosemary's Baby*—Rosemary experiences *dream* versions (that word will be coming up a lot here) of events that later play out in reality. She previews transit between the two apartments' closeted midpoint. Of going to the *Orpheum* to see a film: *". . . only it was live, not a movie."* (Just as "Baby Night" will later prove to have been real, and not a dream.)

Rosemary later regards these foreshadowings as having been God-granted visions: *". . . a sign from heaven, a divine message to be stored away and remembered now for assurance in a time of trial."* In *Son of Rosemary*, she tells Joe/Satan directly: *"I have visions."* (A page later: *"Do you? Have visions?" "Sometimes,"* she said.)

What's happening in both books is not, and *could* not, be mere dreaming, as will be discussed further down. They're *visions*—visions of future trials, coming travails. (Not, ironically, unlike the visitations *Scrooge* receives in *A Christmas Carol*. Spoiler alert: *those* might've been dreams!)

A year after *Son of Rosemary's* 1997 publication, a fan wrote my father, eager to know if their take on the ending was correct. They conjectured that the ending *had* to be written as it was, because, as they'd put it, *"fiction had become non-fiction to fans of Rosemary's Baby."*

Here is my father's reply (shared for the first time): *"You hit the nail right on the head. Son of Rosemary ends the way it does because I'm sorry that Rosemary's Baby encouraged so many people, directly and indirectly, to believe in Satan. The sequel was intended to "deconstruct" the original. I wish more readers (and reviewers!) were as sharp as you are. I congratulate you."*

My father, a lifelong *rationalist*, had hoped that writing *Rosemary's Baby* would make people more skeptical of religious myths in general—that by presenting them in the context of a thriller, they would lose some of their negative power. *"I thought that by dealing with Satan that way, that it would sort of lighten things up—but of course, it didn't. The success of the film, in particular, led to all these other works."* These other works being most notably *The Exorcist* and *The Omen*; and then nearly everything that's followed in the collective "contemporary occult" wake, through the present day. (At the time of this writing, Omen-prequel *The First Omen* just hit screens.)

But alas—as Levin wrote in 2003, *"Two generations of young-sters have grown to adulthood watching depictions of Satan as a living reality."* Televangelism and cable TV infotainment further fueled this surfeit of satanism, contributing to the *Satanic panic* of the 1980s and 1990s—where something as innocuous as *Dungeons & Dragons* was viewed as the Devil's gateway (Though such paranoia-fueled movements are historical mainstays—the Salem witch trials, the *Red Scares, 'QAnon'* . . .). Those who question the foundation of Levin's concern might ponder the outsized role the religious right is playing in our current sociopolitical landscape.

My father was not keen on sequels as a general matter. His *Son*—notes confirm he chose its title, in part, *"for its kidding-the-sequels flavor."* Colleague Peter Straub discerned as much, writing in 2002: *"[N]ot a single reviewer of Son of Rosemary [. . .] understood that [it] satirized the excesses of its own supposed genre."* Perhaps relatedly, my father gave the Devil the impish line: *"Maybe I knew, or just hoped [. . .] that there was the possibility, so to speak, of a sequel for us."*

So—there it is. As a book intended to "deconstruct" its forbear, *Son of Rosemary*'s ending certainly creates the *possibility* that both books' events are purely imaginary.

But stop and consider: How could an *only-dreaming*

Rosemary, back in 1965 (as she is both at the start of *Rose-mary's Baby* and at the end of *Son of Rosemary*), simply *dream* of the later existence of rollerblades? By that name? Video rent-als? The I-heart-New-York device? Or that in 1999 a memorial to John Lennon (down to its circular "IMAGINE" mosaic) would sit in an area of Central Park inaugurated as "Strawberry Fields" *in 1981?*

My father's notes make quite clear that he was eminently mindful of the implications of including references to matters arising after *Rosemary's Baby*'s timeframe (beyond the easily-pre-dicted). He is, after all, the writer Stephen King called *"the Swiss watchmaker of the suspense novel,"* whose plotting *"makes what the rest of us do look like those five-dollar watches you can buy in the discount drugstores."* (He pointed out to his editor for instance that *"Strawberry Fields Forever"* wasn't even *released* until 1967.)

Even *Son*'s ending provides a subtle tip-off that its events *aren't* figmentary—both Joe/Satan and *Hutch* (respectively) use the exact same phrase—first in, then immediately out of, Rosemary's *dream: "three minutes and twelve seconds"* (first in reference to the candles' triggering, then to Hutch's solving of *"Roast Mules"*).

Given its deconstructionist agenda, much as *Rosemary's Baby* scrambled up the letters in *Roman Castevet* to make *Steven Mar-cato, Son of Rosemary* might be thought of as *Rosemary's Baby*'s own anagram—a scrambling-up of *its* component parts; its fun-house-mirror reflection—with the first book's key conflicts, events, and relationships revisited, in an amped-up, stakes-raised manner:

Previously, Rosemary was venerated by the *coven*; here, the *world*. Before, the consequences of her conflicted feelings toward Andy were distant and speculative—there, they *threat-ened* humanity; here, they're immediate and apocalyptic—they *annihilate* it. (And again, she must contemplate the unthinkable—sacrificing Andy to save humanity.) Before, her paramour (Guy) was a *bastard*; here, he (Joe/Satan) is the literal *Devil*. (Though then she followed Satan *figuratively*, here she follows him literally to hell.) And—while Rosemary formerly longed to be Andy's *mother*—she now desires to be his *lover*. (These *are* big themes . . . *Christ/Antichrist, Good/Evil* . . .)

On a structural level, both books are presented in three sections. Rosemary again works in TV production (as her character did *prenarratively* in *Rosemary's Baby*). She joins covens in both works (here, willingly). Her late-book infiltration of the *God's Children* offices is a retracing of her earlier inter-apartment trek (with the new setting's omnipresent *"forest-green"* decor harkening back to the *Bramford's* primordial *"branches"* of hallway, *"walled and carpeted in dark green"*). And God's Children serves as a mordant reversal of Andy's own parentage.

On a smaller scale, while Rosemary had previously promised Andy a nursery without *"one drop of witchy old black,"* here she gifts him a black satin robe (not unlike the one Roman wore on Baby Night.) Japanese *Hayato* returns in the form of *Yuriko*, and Greek *Stavropolous* is hat-tipped in a reference to Hellenic *Melina Mercouri*. Even the famous haircut returns, *"courtesy of the hot new hairdresser,"* with Andy stepping into Guy's shoes both to disapprove, and to bring roses.

While Rosemary previously had to convince Guy to take the apartment, here (at *Son's* end) he's convincing her—as is the formerly *anti-Bramford Hutch*. She watches televised candle-lighting activities from Yankee Stadium, just as Guy earlier watched the Pope's televised Baby Night address from there. The first book's *"fool-nobody"* Santa Clauses return. And while Guy earlier 'transformed' into the Devil, here the Devil transforms into Guy: *"[Joe/Satan] waggled a giant tongue in her face;*

she shut her eyes and screamed, his arms hugging her. "Ro! Ro!" [Guy] cried, holding her, hugging her, kissing her head. 'You're okay! You're okay!'"

Even on the linguistic level, my father invokes *Son*'s predecessor. Rosemary refers to Guy's quip about the identicality of lack-of-fame and death as *"his little joke"*—exactly how *Minnie Castevet* referred thirty-three years earlier to *"Guy's little joke about the Pope."* Sardonic references are also present, such as *"You act as if we're selling* cigarettes*"*—a possible nod to the *Pall Mall* cigarettes Guy had earlier dumped on the kitchen table (the spoils of a TV ad gig).

Deconstruction, however, was not the prime motivation in *Son of Rosemary*'s writing. The biggest factor was my father's realization that *Andrew Woodhouse*—the Antichrist—would be turning thirty-three in 1999—the same age as Christ at his crucifixion and resurrection. And *on the eve of the new millennium*, no less—at the time when the widely-feared *"Y2K problem"* indeed seemed poised to unleash hell across the globe, as all the world's computer systems would simultaneously fail, it was believed. The storytelling appeal was too much for Levin to pass up. He hesitated, though—for the very reasons stated above.

Enter Hollywood mogul Alan Ladd Jr.—who encouraged my father to follow through on writing the book, with a promise to film it using a Levin-penned screenplay, and with untold creative control over its casting, and all other key creative considerations. Needless to say, that film never materialized. (Sometimes a dream *is* just a dream.)

In 2004, the television series rights, which my father had retained in the original 1968 film contract, were optioned for a much-desired melding of *Rosemary's Baby* and *Son of Rosemary*. Some legal jockeying by Paramount over their own rights resulted in a ten-year time window being imposed on the project's release, and—the matter changing hands once or twice during the ensuing period—a hastily-undertaken version was ultimately released in 2014, just before the referenced window's expiration, limited in scope to the first book alone.

Returning to the books themselves, *Rosemary's Baby*—seismically—inverted the story of Jesus's birth; the *Savior* hung *literally* upside-down, suspended over Andrew John Woodhouse's black bassinet. With Rosemary serving as the antithesis of the biblical Mary (a *non*-virgin, *non*-believer). Her ultimate decision—to *spare* her baby—subjected humanity to the birth of the Antichrist. She knew this was the wrong choice—hence her initial impulse on seeing her child for the first time: *"The thing to do was kill it. Obviously. [. . .] Save the world from God-knows-what. From Satan-knows-what."*

Rosemary reasoned that—aside from killing being wrong itself—she could steer Andy in the right direction, and counter the coven's influence. *Son . . .* finds her *partly* right in that—Andy *does* finally try to disclose the *Lighting's* true purpose to her—albeit after concealing it at length (betraying her trust—just as Guy had).

Imperfect though Rosemary's early decision was, my father still viewed it as a triumph for her, on a personal level: she'd rescued her son and wrested control from the coven—from the very Devil himself.

By contrast, Terry Gionoffrio *refused* to participate in the coven's designs—leading to her death (whether by her own hand, or that of the coven—my father left that open to readerly interpretation).

This contrast between Terry and Rosemary actually informs a seemingly incidental detail in *Rosemary's Baby*: on first meeting Terry, Rosemary mistakes her for the actress and singer *Anna Maria Alberghetti*. Later, the culminating image of Rosemary's six-page *dream* sequence consists of Alberghetti (read: Terry) sitting inside the Pope's ring: *"He held out his hand for her to kiss the ring. Its stone was a silver filigree ball less than an inch in diameter; inside it, very tiny, Anna Maria Alberghetti sat waiting."* For what is Terry *waiting*? For *Rosemary*, I'd propose. For her to make the same *humanity-affirming* choice as Terry did, and join her on the *path of righteousness,* at the Pope's side. (One of my brothers in fact recalls my father half-joking that the new book gave Rosemary *"another chance to get it right."*)

Note how Alberghetti's name sneaks in the Latin form of "Mary"—*Maria.* Rosemary mistakes Terry for—well, *herself*—because she recognizes in Terry her own *God-willed* fate. That's my take, at least.

Rosemary's *Andy-or-Humanity* dilemma is carried over into *Son of Rosemary.* Now wishing (as above) to be more than mother to the half-human/half-divine Andy—Rosemary allows her guilt over that fact to blind her to humankind's imminent demise: *"[Rosemary] wept. If she had come up here Wednesday night, when she had first heard Andy calling . . . If she had not had her guilt to confuse her . . ."*

Dream or no dream, what *Son of Rosemary's* ending does, on a purely mechanical level, is to shunt Rosemary back to the start of the first book, at which point both books' events will presumably begin repeating themselves. You could argue that these earlier *visions* would serve to inoculate Rosemary against any coming repetitions. But remember, she had her share of premonitory warnings on offer the *first* time around—and look how *that* turned out. Further—while *Son of Rosemary's* entire plot is set into motion through the killing of Dr. Shand by a divinely-guided taxi—Rosemary fails to make the post-*dream* connection that her house-sitting opportunity is the result of the intended sitter getting *hit by a taxi* a day earlier. (And that's *after* Rosemary prays to God over his possibly having *"had a hand in Stan Shand dying when he did, so I would wake up and do something You want to be done."*)

My personal, pet theory—and it's only that—is that this *dream-dream-repeat* pattern will play (or already *is* playing) out repeatedly, in a sort of grand, dual-book 'loop'—with Rosemary stuck in her own *Pilgrim's Progress*—a spiritual *Groundhog Day.* Perpetually tested as part of *"the endless game"* Joe/Satan describes, until she finally chooses light over darkness, Good over Evil—and Humanity over her own earthly interests.

It's worth noting that the initial idea for *Rosemary's Baby* was rooted, to a degree, in the notion of "cyclicality." It arose at a 1960 lecture my father attended on *cycles* in all phases of human life: *"I don't know what was said that gave me the idea, but as soon as I got out of that lecture I jotted down a note about a woman being pregnant with an unnatural fetus."* (You can see this note in the IraLevin.org feature *"Rosemary's Baby Album."*)

Son of Rosemary, just as it happens, is rife with 'circular' symbolism—from its *Columbus Circle* setting (and its cylindrical elevator), to the candles' twin concentric rings, to the circular Lennon memorial. Even Judy's faux *bindi* is itself a tiny circle. And Rosemary has this exchange, for example, with Yuriko (vis-a-vis his circular silver necklace): *"Does it have a special significance?"* [. . .] *"I don't know what the designer intended; to me it suggests life's continuity, the continuity of all things."* (Even the solution to the *Rose Mary*–resonant *Roast Mules* anagram describes a *circular* transit.)

Ultimately—whether the path at hand is circular, linear, or otherwise—*Son of Rosemary* finds Rosemary Riley no closer to joining Terry Gionoffrio beside the Holy Father.

My *own* father knew that reaction to his sequel would be mixed, commenting pre-publication: *"I don't know how audiences are going to react, because it has an edge to it, as far as I'm con-cerned."* It's with perhaps a devilish wink that—in her early Central Park carriage ride (a pre-midnight *Cinderella?)* he has an enraptured Rosemary announce: *"I'm dreaming."*

Nicholas Levin
New York City
July, 2024